BOOK NEWS

Sign up for exclusive updates and offers at
news.jljarvis.com

THE RED ROSE

THE RED ROSE

A MODERN SCOTTISH ROMANCE

J.L. JARVIS

BOOKBINDER PRESS

THE RED ROSE
A Modern Scottish Romance

Published by Bookbinder Press
bookbinderpress.com

ISBN (ebook) 978-1-942767-59-6
ISBN (paperback) 978-1-942767-60-2
ISBN (Barnes & Noble paperback) 979-8-3196-0767-6

I f it hadn't been raining, they might never have met. But it was Scotland. They didn't stand a chance.

Olivia Boyd sat at a desk in the Edinburgh Central Library, tapping away at her keyboard. She'd been in Edinburgh for only three days, but the reference library was already one of her favorite haunts. There was something transcendent about settling down at one of the wooden desks arranged in neat rows and plugging her laptop into the floor outlet under her desk. Except for today. She'd forgotten the cord, but she'd still settled in and lost herself in her work.

She looked up again to find hours had passed. Leaning back in her chair, she gazed at the rows of massive windows framing the sky. On either side, each window overlooked an alcove formed by book stacks twelve shelves high. Halfway up, an iron-railed walkway provided access to the top six shelves. It was an impressive monument to Victorian grandeur and philanthropist-robber-baron Andrew Carnegie's wealth. The ambiance bolstered Olivia. Whether it would drive her dissertation forward was yet to be seen, but she was being productive, which was an improvement over the past several months. She hoped her advisor was right and that a semester abroad would breathe life into her foundering dissertation.

It had to.

YOU'RE DOING IT AGAIN. She wondered if she had some bizarre form of narcolepsy in which, rather than sleeping, she daydreamed. Her whole reason for coming to Scotland was to distance herself from the past and start fresh. She stood, strolled to the opposite side of the library, and returned to her seat somewhat refreshed. Despite an occasional lapse in concentration, she had been more productive since arriving in Edinburgh. If Scotland couldn't inspire her to write about Scottish folk music, it was hopeless—a possibility she hadn't yet ruled out.

She took a breath, exhaled, and refocused her attention on her laptop, which went blank. Dismayed, she stared at the screen. The battery was dead. She gazed up at the looming windows and sighed. Dark clouds drifted by. She glanced at her watch. Four thirty was too early for sunset.

It made sense, though, once she reached the exit and looked through the windows. A storm had moved in, bringing rain that now drummed a relentless cadence on the sidewalk outside. She reached into her bag for her umbrella, but it wasn't there... because it was home, propped up by the door. *Great.* First her power cord and now the umbrella. Pulling up the hood of her raincoat, she headed outside and through the large wrought iron gate. It was only a ten-minute walk to her apartment on the Quartermile by the University of Edinburgh campus. She would get soaked, but she would make it.

While hurrying, she dreamed of getting out of the rain and into her apartment. She walked past the entrance gate to Greyfriars Kirkyard, which was famously haunted, something Olivia had no trouble believing at the moment. Amid the brooding clouds, windswept branches, and rain-drenched mausoleums, she wouldn't have been surprised to encounter a wandering specter or two. Terrified, yes. But surprised? No.

Just off the main road, amber light spilled out through the windows of The Red Rose, an old pub recommended by Dr. McNabb for its music. More important than that, at the moment, it promised dryness and warmth. The crackling fire in a small wood stove drew her farther inside, where the smoke from the fire mixed with the aroma of beer. She stepped farther in, past several tables along the wall across from the bar. The back corner housed a well-worn upright piano on a slightly raised area that served as a stage. From it, she could practically hear echoes of old Scottish folk songs.

She glanced about for a seat. Since arriving in Scotland, she'd been very frugal, eating soup and prepared meals from the Sainsbury's local food shop downstairs in her building. She was due, she decided, for a splurge on a pint and some pub grub.

The after-work crowd inside was lively for a Tuesday. Like Olivia, they'd likely sought refuge from the rain on their way home. The barking laughter of a cluster of men and women near the bar mingled with the murmuring voices that hung in the air.

Movement on the opposite wall drew her attention. At a table beside a small wood stove, a pair of university students stood, zipped up their jackets, and donned book-laden backpacks. No one nearby seemed to have noticed them vacating their table, so Olivia worked her way over and hovered. The instant they stepped away, she slipped into a chair, shrugged off her jacket, and draped it over the chair back. Having staked her claim to the table, she hesitated to move. She felt lost and alone in a new place far from home but resisted the urge to retreat to her familiar apartment. After spending several evenings there, she craved company. Even if she wasn't with them, the energy of the patrons spilled over onto her, and the wood stove warmed her.

Determined to stay, she went to the bar and studied the chalkboard menu while she waited to order. A petite young woman, perhaps in her twenties, slipped past her and joined the bartender, pulling pints one after the other. With her black curls pulled back into a short bun, she whispered to her coworker, her eyes dancing. Olivia didn't hear what prompted her mood shift, but she glared at a gray-bearded patron and said something that made him shrink back.

Olivia studied the man as her imagination filled in the blanks. His face was weathered, and his thin silver hair was confined by a cap. His clothes looked as though they'd taken root unhindered by laundry detergent. No one went to work looking like that. He had to be unemployed or, given his obvious age, retired. He'd offended the female worker; that much was clear. Olivia became so engrossed in her musings that she didn't notice the male bartender now standing before her.

"What'll you have?"

Startled, she turned to him and was startled anew. She had never been easily charmed by appearance alone, but with no apparent effort, he rendered her flustered. He glanced back to the bar with a hint of impatience, which was understandable, given how busy the bar was. But his eyes held her attention. Their kaleidoscope of deep blues, laser-focused on her, made her heart skip a beat.

Olivia regained her composure in time, she hoped, to avoid appearing like she'd never seen a good-looking man before—which wasn't the case at all. He had simply pivoted quickly and surprised her. Anyone would have reacted the same. It had nothing to do with that dark, lustrous mass of controlled chaos on his head, his high cheekbones, strong jawline, or full lips.

Those meant nothing to her. Of course, she was deluding herself. There was something about him, and he wasn't alone. Since arriving in Edinburgh, she'd observed something about Scottish men. From taxi drivers to store clerks, the men of all ages projected a cheerful demeanor with an underlying current of grit that she found very manly. Anyone who might accuse her of overgeneralizing could take a ten-minute walk and tally the masculine men they encountered. She wondered if it was in their DNA, a genetic memory of hard times passed down through generations. The women had their own version. Everyone she'd encountered was unerringly warm, but Olivia had the distinct sense that if put to the test, they wouldn't put up with nonsense. She liked that about them. It was possible her impressions were skewed by the exhilaration of being in Scotland. She loved it—the country, the history, the architecture, and most of all, the people.

That included the bartender, who was north of six feet tall and not overly bulky. She approved of his corded forearm muscles and the broad set of his shoulders. *And that is a penetrating stare.*

Because he's waiting for you! So stop gawking and order! The man's busy!

His eyes darted away.

Extremely busy. She tried to be quick. "A half-pint and a bowl of Cullen skink."

He had the pleasant but expectant look of a man trying to hide his impatience. "A half-pint of what?"

Uh... I don't know! She felt like she was failing a test. "Beer?"

He glanced past the half dozen taps that lined his side of the bar to a man with a twenty-pound note in hand, waiting to order. "Give it some thought. I'll be back."

While she intended to mull it over, she became distracted as he walked away. Worried she might lose her table or jacket, she glanced over, but both were still there. She refocused on her beer choices, but the names and logos meant nothing to her.

He returned. "Have you decided?"

She hated wasting his time, but she was at a loss. "I'm not much of a beer drinker. What do you recommend?"

"Let's narrow it down. Light beer or dark?"

She shook her head. She was more of a wine drinker, but no one had a glass of wine in hand. Apparently, people here went to a pub for a pint, so she felt compelled to try it.

He lifted an eyebrow. She wasn't sure how to interpret that. "Wait there." He went to the taps and returned with two small glasses of beer—one dark and one light. "Try these." He disappeared.

Olivia tasted each. When he returned, she pointed to a glass. "I like the dark one."

He nodded approvingly then pulled her a half-pint of the dark beer.

"What is it? In case I want to order it again."

"Dark Island."

She made a mental note of it then asked, "And my soup?"

"We'll bring it to your table."

Olivia paid him and went back to her table. She sat, leaning her shoulder against the dark-wood wainscoting that rose to meet red plaster walls. As she soaked in the fire's warmth and the room's conversational murmur, an inexplicable sensation of coming home settled upon her. It made no sense, but the feeling was too strong to deny. She took a sip of her beer and leaned back, wholly content.

She had made the right choice. Being in Scotland would revive a career that had gone off the rails. She'd begun her PhD work well enough but lost control of it somewhere around the beginning of her fourth year at Cornell. On a sunny morning the previous June, her mother had gone out to the backyard to work in the garden. Halfway across the lawn, she stopped and turned. Olivia looked through the kitchen window at her mother's pained eyes and set down the coffeepot.

Surrounded by flowers and grass, she stood as if frozen in time then collapsed on the lawn.

The semester that followed was a foggy memory of plodding along, making excuses for her lack of progress. She spent hours in the library, sheet music fanned out on the table before her while her eyes strayed to the window. Outside, everyone else seemed to walk with a purpose from building to building, no doubt accomplishing more than she was. Instead, she hid away wearing headphones and listening to old scratchy recordings of Celtic songs, pen in hand, her wrist resting idly on a blank spiral notebook.

Why? She asked it a lot. *Why ethnomusicology? Why can't I stop grieving?* Things she hadn't thought of in years drifted up to the surface: fleeting snapshots of childhood memories of sun-splashed days in the park with her parents, her father's hand grasping hers, and shuffling along a frozen creek in her double-runner ice skates. Then her father had left them, and part of her mother had left too. The next couple of years were a blur, with a few scattered memories long since detached from the days they belonged to. By the time Olivia reached high school, she and her mother had outgrown the sad years. Life was good. But now, that life was over.

The spring semester ended, and Olivia was the same distracted shell of a student who'd begun the year mired in research, still rewriting the same twenty pages she couldn't seem to get past. And then she met Noah.

"Cullen skink." The bartender set down a thick white china bowl filled with chowder.

"Thank you." The fish smell was robust.

She must have reacted visibly to it, because his eyebrows drew together. "Have you had it before?"

"No, but it looks amazing."

He looked doubtful. "It's fishy."

She nodded. "I thought I detected a faint seafood aroma."

His eyes twinkled. "Did you now?"

She laughed, and he joined in.

He seemed to take pity on her. "I can get you something else."

"No! I'll have this." She gave him an insistent look.

The warmth in his eyes lit his face. That was a new look for him. She didn't mind it at all. A few minutes ago, she wouldn't have guessed he even had a smile, let alone such a winning one. As he returned to the bar, she was still pondering it, along with his deep Scottish burr. She could listen to that all day long, the mellow tones of his Scottish brogue, velvety rolling R's, and lilting phrasing. A voice like that could read bedtime stories to her, but she doubted she would sleep. Her mind wandered, but she reeled it back in. No, that voice would never grow old.

She wasn't alone in her opinion of the accent. Before leaving home, she'd noticed Scottish accents popping up in TV commercials. Now, here she was, surrounded by them. She sighed and soaked it all in. *What a great place to be.*

The bartender turned back toward her. Only then did she realize she was staring. Just in time, she looked away toward the fire. No matter which way she turned, it was hot. She stopped short of fanning herself like an antebellum ingenue.

What's the matter with you? You are better than this.

But was she? Maybe people just said that because, deep down, they knew they weren't.

Dismissing the thought, Olivia picked up her spoon and dipped it into the Cullen skink. It was intensely fishy—and delicious. She glanced toward the bar and locked eyes with the bartender. The heat of a blush filled her cheeks. Something shifted within her, as though the world had gone on spinning and left them behind.

A loud shout rose from the bar. "Hey, Max! Gie us a pint!"

His eyes darted toward a man holding up an empty pint glass. Max gave him a nod and tossed a glance back in Olivia's direction before leaving.

Max. He looked like a Max. Olivia didn't date his type —rugged physique, chiseled face, and deep-set eyes. She had nothing against good-looking men, but she'd met a few. College campuses were crawling with them, and like so many grocery store pastries, they never turned out to be as good as they looked. At this point in life, her late twenties, if someone like that showed an interest in her, she was wise enough to know it would never work out. Or she used to be.

Hmm. That was a definite glance. He was probably just watching to see how I reacted to the soup.

She watched him walk away until a bar patron shifted his stance and obstructed her view. *Dang it!* That shouldn't have annoyed her as much as it did. But, in all fairness, it was her view, and he'd blocked it. She was pretty sure men brawled over less at sporting events.

So, his name was Max. *Max... Maximilian?*

Maxim? Maxwell? He looked like he could be a Maxwell. Her interest was purely academic, of course. It was all about context. As a student of Scottish music and culture, as well as an observant tourist of sorts, she would be remiss in failing to make note of the locals. That's what travel was about—not just seeing the sights but also making connections.

That was all she was doing—connecting with Max, on a purely informational basis. Some people kept travel journals. She made detailed mental notes.

Olivia was, after all, an observer. It was her academic duty to soak it all in. She was nothing if not a professional—a professional student, but still... If universities could engage in ridiculous studies like "Tree Climbing" or "How to Watch Television," she could do her own irrelevant research. At the moment, she was making an informal study of forest-green flannel shirts, blue jeans, and Doc Martens, as well as the intriguing men who wore them. At their first meeting, her dissertation advisor had cautioned that there came a point when the research had to stop. Olivia wasn't there yet.

She reminded herself that Max wasn't her type. *Why is that again?* She failed to come up with a rational reason. All she could think of was that Max was unique. The campus she'd just left had some good-looking guys, but they were nothing like Max. It wasn't simply the accent, although, to be honest, that did tip the scales in his favor. Perhaps it was the way he walked across the room with the effortless grace of a man who didn't worry about what people thought. Of course that would appeal to her because he had what she lacked—

complete ease in social settings, along with a clear sense of his place in the world.

When Olivia's schoolwork cratered, the confidence she'd once enjoyed had gone with it. No longer sure of herself, she felt adrift. Career websites weren't teeming with jobs for ethnomusicologists with incomplete doctorates in traditional Scottish folk music. So she had followed her heart, which didn't seem to care about paying the bills.

Her heart knew what it wanted, and at the moment, her heart hummed in Max's presence. She couldn't help herself. She blamed Scotland. This would never have happened in New York. But Edinburgh was enchanting, and nothing felt real.

Now desperate to be disenchanted, she applied logic to break free of its spell. So what if Max was confident? Lots of people were. Olivia, herself, used to be. She was intelligent, focused, and hardworking. Those qualities had gotten her a graduate teaching assistantship at a university she wouldn't otherwise have been able to afford. But that was school. This was real life, where her discomfort went deeper. Maybe Max's confidence had never been tested like hers. Worse yet, maybe this was the tip of the iceberg. Confidence was a double-edged sword. Successful people possessed it, but jerks did too. She wondered where Max fell on that spectrum.

She returned to her soup. She was overthinking things. That was a pitfall of being alone, but she would adjust. All that mattered right now was this charming Scottish pub, the cozy fire beside her, and the hot chowder before her.

When she'd finished her soup, she leaned back,

sipped her beer, and left all thought behind. When it couldn't have seemed any more perfect, the crowd thinned, improving her view of Max. Until now, she wouldn't have thought dark wavy hair was her favorite, but now, she couldn't imagine anything better.

The guy didn't smile much, but when he did, he was excellent at it. He manned the bar with the deftness of a professional plate spinner, keeping everything turning, including her head. He wasn't prone to banal banter with patrons, but he chatted enough to keep them smiling and drinking. Now that was an art. He turned toward Olivia, but she averted her eyes just in time.

Do you know what isn't an art? Looking cool while staring at bartenders like a lost puppy.

Max wasn't entirely perfect. His face was a bit asymmetrical. He had frown lines between his eyebrows, although he didn't seem like a scowler. Maybe he was a deep thinker—a philosophical bartender. His day's growth of beard might have been a little uneven. She couldn't tell from this far away.

Stop squinting. It's not like you've been tasked with deciding where he falls on a scale of one to ten.

Nine.

No one was ever a ten. It was Olivia's way of managing her expectations. But Max was attractive, and that was enough.

Enough for what? Olivia had a boyfriend—well, she used to.

2

His name was Noah, and he used to be perfect for her. He was the boyfriend version of a favorite sweater—well-worn and comfortable when needed and slung over a desk chair when not. Olivia frowned. That wasn't fair. Noah meant more to her than that. They were practically in love, although they'd never said it in so many words. But after a year, it was clear they were headed that way. They were comfortable and seldom disagreed, and they'd put in the time. If they weren't in love yet, they would get there.

Except they wouldn't now, because they were on "a break." Olivia kept forgetting that. "A break" sounded deceptively temporary, but she knew better than that. They'd had some heated discussions—a lot of discussions—some loud. Noah had found so many reasons for her not to go to Scotland that tension had mounted between them. By the time she'd left, even though Noah called it a break, it was more like a truce. At first, it was a relief. Everything she used to rely on, the comfort and ease they'd once shared, was now cracked and crumbling like an eggshell clinging hopelessly to its membrane long after the damage was done.

It was going to end. They just needed to go through this dance of semantics, sidestepping around their coughing and wheezing relationship, watching it slowly expire. Only then would they call it the end, by which time it would be so far beyond obvious that feeling nothing would be a relief. Even so, she would miss the little things they'd once done together, like grocery shopping and stopping for Friday-night pizza before going home to watch movies. She'd once viewed them as special couple traditions, although, looking back, they were just errands and routines.

Noah was a great guy. Like Olivia, he had a tireless work ethic, and neither of them liked drama. His methodical diligence had sent him up the corporate ladder from stock boy to corporate regional manager of a grocery store chain. With a shelf full of career self-help books to show for it, he had studied the social norms that would best set him on his desired career trajectory. He had mastered the business-casual look to a tee with his trimmed hair, pressed chinos, sports coat, and shirt with no tie. A faint scent wafted around him— Irish Spring, Old Spice, and Crest or, as Olivia liked to think of it, grocery aisle seven.

Noah was a man of few words, and all of them prac-tical. Everything he owned, he packed away neatly or arranged to perfection. Olivia had once discovered a list of clothing he wore in a two-week rotation taped to the inside of his closet door. That was Noah. Proper organi-zation required no further thought. And with the addition of Olivia in his life, every piece of his life had been assembled: food and shelter, a steady job, and a reliable girlfriend.

Noah and Max couldn't have been more opposite—not that she knew anything about Max. But he seemed intriguingly different. The only thing Max seemed to have in common with Noah was height. But Noah had the slender frame of a weekend cyclist, while Max had more of a rugby physique. She wasn't sure what a rugby physique was. She'd never even been to a game. *Or do they call it a match?* Either way, rugby just sounded burlier. Add to that some disheveled dark hair and a day's growth of beard, and that was Max. In the opposite corner was Noah—fine-boned build, trimmed blond hair, and a face that had never seen a five-o'clock shadow.

And Max is the bartender—a stranger who's nothing to you. Noah is—was—your boyfriend. Olivia exhaled. She should have felt something more than ambivalence. Of course, she would miss him, but after leaving to live across the ocean, what she felt most of all was free. And that made her feel guilty.

People liked Noah. They couldn't help it. She'd never known anyone so unerringly tactful. She used to wonder how he did it. So it had come as a shock when, upon hearing her plans for Scotland, he'd revealed a new side to his character—seething with resentment.

Noah was a planner, and they'd never even talked about Scotland. Yet somehow, Olivia had gone to see her dissertation advisor for a regular meeting and come out with a startling plan—her plan, not Noah's.

PROFESSOR DENISE LAMANSKI'S office looked nothing like the bare, white-walled classrooms where she usually taught. One wall of her office was lined with bookshelves packed with vertically arranged books. A desk covered in stacks of books, papers, and a desktop computer faced a tall window. Behind it, facing the door, was a table with two guest chairs. One chair contained a disheveled pile of books topped with a foot-tall stack of file folders. The wall space was filled with diplomas, pictures, and art prints, giving an impression of knowledge, culture, and comfort. Dr. Lamanski was at her desk with her back to the door. Olivia hesitated then knocked lightly on the open door.

Without turning to look, her advisor said, "Come in."

Olivia quietly made her way to the one empty chair, where she sat, and she waited. It couldn't have been more than a minute, but it seemed like five.

Dr. Lamanski pivoted in her chair. "Olivia. Hello." She rolled her chair a few inches closer to the table, facing Olivia. The professor had the look of a grandmother, the mind of a computer, and a tireless work ethic that no one could match. She smiled. "How are you?"

"I'm fine, thank you."

"Good." Her pleasant demeanor looked forced. She took a moment. "There's no easy way to say this. Your teaching assistantship is not being renewed."

Olivia's stomach sank.

"I know it's disappointing. But it might be a blessing in disguise."

Olivia wasn't feeling blessed at the moment, but she

still had her dignity. On second thought, the way Dr. Lamanski's shoulders slumped and her face filled with pity, Olivia realized that was gone too.

Dr. Lamanski held up a finger. "All is not lost!"

Great. I'm feeling better already. Don't wince. Don't frown, either. Pretend you've had Botox.

"Let's look at the plus side. With no classes to teach and no papers to grade, you can focus on your dissertation." Dr. Lamanski opened her laptop. "Which brings us to this." She slid the laptop around at an angle so Olivia could view the latest draft she'd turned in a few days before. The column containing her professor's comments looked longer than the draft she'd submitted.

Her advisor removed her glasses and set them on the table. "Olivia, let's talk about this."

Olivia was mortified. She hadn't expected the feedback to be glowing, but she'd hoped it wouldn't be so painful. Tension clamped her throat. She couldn't speak.

Dr. Lamanski broke the unbearable silence. "How would you... assess the status of your work at this point?"

She didn't have to say more. Olivia managed a nod to her advisor's questioning look. She had to say something. "I know it's... undeveloped."

The only response she received was a raised eyebrow.

"It's not ready, I know. But... we were due to touch base and..." Olivia lifted her hands as she shrugged helplessly.

"It's been five years."

Olivia knew that. Two other students who'd started

at the same time had already graduated. And here she was, not even close to finished. She'd become another ABD—all but the dissertation. Her professor looked pained, but not nearly as pained as Olivia felt.

"I fought for you, but I couldn't produce any signs of progress..." Dr. Lamanski paused, brow furrowed. "You're a smart woman. You're well aware of how important this is." She stared at Olivia as though she were unaware. "This document establishes your professional credibility and that of your doctoral degree."

Olivia was acutely aware. She knew she wasn't performing. Like a pro athlete, she'd been cut from the team.

As if she'd given up waiting for an explanation from Olivia, Dr. Lamanski glanced at the screen displaying Olivia's work and waved her hand toward it. The dismissive gesture hurt almost as much as her words. "Why didn't you come to me sooner?"

Olivia swallowed. Why couldn't she just sink into the floor here and now and just vanish, let the earth swallow her beneath layers of despair and a few feet of topsoil? "I didn't want you to see it until it was ready. I know it's not. I guess I thought if I just did a little more research, I'd find something—that one thing—that would make everything fall into place. And the teaching took more of my time than I expected." *Just like this lame explanation.*

Dr. Lamanski had a way of looking both sympathetic and demanding. At the moment, the latter was on full display. With a furrowed brow, the professor gave her head a helpless shake. "I've seen what you're capable of."

And this isn't it. She'd left that part out, most likely because it was obvious. Olivia knew that before she'd walked into the meeting, but hearing it from her revered mentor made it hurt all the more. "I'm sorry."

"Don't apologize to me. You're letting yourself down. You can do better."

Olivia nodded, unable to speak through the lump in her throat.

Dr. Lamanski's eyes softened. "Are you sure you want to continue with the program?"

"Yes!"

"There's no shame if—"

"I want to!" That sounded desperate. She drew in a breath. "I really want to continue."

"I'm glad to hear it. I wasn't sure."

"I am! I absolutely want to finish! I can do better!" *Now you're just sounding pathetic.*

"Okay. Well, let's see what we can do." She pulled the laptop closer. "I've written some notes."

Olivia nodded.

The professor seemed to change her mind and slid the laptop aside. "Before we get into the weeds, let's look at the big picture. I think you should narrow your topic. Celtic folk music is a fantastic area to study, but there's so much. The Celtic culture spans the globe. There are so many aspects of it."

"I know! The more I kept digging, the more I found that I just couldn't ignore. Did you know they still have *cèilidhs* in parts of Canada? Generations after migrating there, they still cling to the music and dance of their ancestors. But then, in the Appalachian mountains, the old songs remained almost unchanged for decades and decades. They were still singing medieval ballads from Scotland at the turn of the twentieth century, but dancing at *cèilidhs* seemed to fall by the wayside. Or maybe they didn't. I'm not finding any references to them, but I need to research that more. What I'm finding is clog dancing and step dancing. But wouldn't that be more Irish than Scottish?"

Dr. Lamanski considered the question. But before she could answer, Olivia shrugged it off. "In any event, it's in America that Scottish music changes. The outside world starts to seep into the isolated mountain communities. Mountain music was changed forever by African rhythms, spirituals, and eventually rhythm and blues, leading to the birth of country music. In one sense, the world is encroaching upon the old ways, and yet, faced with the threat of modern culture and politics, the mountain communities weave it all in almost seamlessly. And it doesn't stop there. I mean, look at the industrial revolution. Out of the horrible conditions of the coal mines and factories grow protest songs—a theme that's picked up with force in the sixties. I mean, would there even have been a Bob Dylan without Scottish music?"

Without waiting for an answer, Olivia continued. "But then, is that really an issue of direct influence, or could it be generational?" Olivia waved her wrist toward the screen. "There's a reference there somewhere in my notes about generational memory. Maybe there's something in Bob Dylan's ancestry—or Woody Guthrie's or Pete Seeger's—that stems from genetic memory fused into their DNA."

Olivia drew in a breath, but Professor Lamanski held up her palms. "Whoa! Hold on."

Olivia stopped short. "Oh! I'm sorry. I guess I got carried away."

Dr. Lamanski looked at her frankly. "Never apologize for your passion. That and knowledge will get you very far in this field. To be honest, I'm happy to see it."

At that moment, Olivia felt she'd returned to the comfortable footing she'd enjoyed in her first year of doctoral study.

"However..."

The moment was gone. Olivia's discomfort returned.

Her advisor pointed at the rough draft on the laptop. "I'm not seeing that same passion in here. You've just rattled off the seeds of a half dozen dissertations. By the way, Bob Dylan's ancestors were from Ukraine, which takes us all the way across Europe. But Eastern European music, in particular Jewish music, has had an enormous effect on American music as well. Look at the musical theater! And you bring up a riveting topic with genetic memory. But for a dissertation on that, you'd need to dig into the science. How's your biology background?"

Olivia winced.

Dr. Lamanski smiled. "And here we are, back to the problem—focus. Your draft seems to hover primarily around Scotland. Shall we stick with that?"

Olivia nodded.

"Good. So... Scotland. There's still a lot there." She regarded Olivia. "You look confused."

"No. Well, yes. Sort of. I get it. I need to narrow my topic. I'm just not sure how."

Dr. Lamanski pulled the laptop closer and pointed

to the screen. "What I'm seeing so far are a lot of rabbit trails that lead in different directions."

Exactly! Olivia wanted to sigh with relief. Or cry. She did neither. Instead, she caught herself nodding like a bobblehead.

Dr. Lamanski leveled a steady gaze over her glasses. "They're all interesting trails. Which one would you like to go down?"

Olivia drew in a breath but felt a sudden loss for words.

"Let me ask you this. What initially drew you to Celtic music?"

Olivia hesitated. "Well, it's not very academic."

"That's okay. We're just fishing right now. So what if we reel in an old shoe? We'll just throw it back and try again." She smiled warmly.

"Okay. Well, I love the music—always have. My mother's ancestors were from Scotland. She had an old photo album dating back to the early 1900s. One picture showed an old couple sitting on a porch. The man had a fiddle, and the woman's mouth was open as if she was singing. I wondered how it sounded."

Dr. Lamanski nodded. "That's good. Could you narrow it further?"

Olivia frowned and stared off into the distance. "By the purpose—like for singing or dancing?"

"Go on."

"Well, people sang ballads to tell a story. There was other music for dancing, which brings up instrumentation. Did you know that the hand drum or bodhrán wasn't even considered a musical instrument until the 1960s? It was only then that it became associated with Celtic folk music. But back to the Appalachians, they were really inventive. Look what they did with spoons, and they created a bass from a washtub."

Dr. Lamanski's eyes twinkled.

Olivia wrinkled her nose. "Another rabbit trail?"

"Not necessarily. Although instrumentation might be a little too narrow. I'm a bit out of my wheelhouse here, but aside from necessity being the mother of invention, wasn't the instrumentation also driven by who happened to attend any given occasion and what instrument they played?"

"True."

"Remind me. What was your undergraduate major?"

"Voice... Oh! I could focus on songs. The instruments are still a factor worth discussing, but the songs and the stories they tell would be interesting to explore —and to trace from their roots." She envisioned that old family photo and the curiosity it'd sparked. "Appalachian folk music and its Scottish origins!"

Her advisor's eyes lit up. "I like it!"

Olivia felt her world come into focus. "From Scotland to Appalachia. That's a journey I'd love to go on." Slowly, she said it again, as if trying it on like a garment. "From Scotland to Appalachia: A Journey in Song."

"And wouldn't it be easier traveling that journey on one road instead of several roads at the same time?"

Olivia nodded. There might as well have been a choir of angels, Olivia felt so elated.

They were basking in the victory when Dr. Lamanski exclaimed, "Scotland!"

"Yes...?" Olivia was confused. They had agreed on Scotland several minutes before. Maybe it was some sort of delayed reaction or senior moment.

"Excuse me a minute." With no explanation, her advisor quickly got up and walked out of the office.

Olivia heard voices down the hall but couldn't make out what they were saying. Dr. Lamanski reappeared with a colleague in tow. "Dr. Mary McNabb, this is Olivia Boyd. She's doing her dissertation on Scottish folk songs."

Dr. McNabb's face lit up. "Excellent choice!"

Her advisor turned to Olivia. "Dr. McNabb is a visiting professor from the University of Edinburgh."

Now that was something Olivia felt comfortable talking about. "I love Edinburgh!"

Dr. McNabb's face brightened. "You've been there?"

"Just once. I took a train up from London and spent one afternoon there. I loved it!"

"One afternoon? That's not nearly enough!"

"I know!"

Dr. Lamanski said, "Dr. McNabb told me earlier that her Edinburgh sublet fell through at the last minute. So I thought of you."

Dr. McNabb said, "It's right by the university. You know, Edinburgh has dozens of pubs with live traditional music. You could stay at my flat, research by day, and listen to live music at night. There are libraries and museums within a short walk—and the culture! Some of those pubs are centuries old! Just imagine yourself sitting and listening to the same music performed in the same old historic taverns for hundreds of years. It would give you such a rich wealth of experience to draw from for your dissertation. And you should definitely take a few side trips to the Highlands."

Olivia couldn't believe what she was hearing, but

reality soon set in. "That sounds amazing! But I don't know if I can afford it."

"Oh, I'm not asking for rent. I just need someone to house-sit."

"But..." This couldn't be happening to her. "Why?"

Dr. McNabb smiled. "You don't get through this life without help. I had help to get through school. Now I'm able to help someone else."

"I... I don't know what to say."

Dr. Lamanski's eyes sparkled. "I'd say yes."

Olivia's head started spinning with numbers. "I'd love to do it! Can I let you know tomorrow?"

"Absolutely." Dr. McNabb glanced at her watch. "I've got a class now. Stop by my office in the morning, and we can talk more."

Olivia's advisor sat down and leaned her elbows on the table. "You've had a rough go of it so far, but I believe in your potential. Scotland could be just what you need."

Still dumbstruck, Olivia said, "I want to go! But I need to work out some details."

Dr. Lamanski went on as though it were decided. "You and I can do all our meetings via video confer-ence. I'll pick Dr. McNabb's brain for some resources there to get you off to a strong start." She hesitated and, with a serious tone, added, "This might be the perfect impetus to get you to the finish line."

Ouch. The professor's "impetus" felt like a kick in the pants. She couldn't deny that she'd lost control of not only her dissertation but also her life.

Shortly after she met Noah, her time management skills had circled the drain. She couldn't blame it on Noah. She'd latched on to him like a lifesaver, as though he'd pull her back onboard the ship. But he didn't pull her back. He dragged her along on his own journey, wanting to spend all their free time together. Others went to school and maintained relationships, but Olivia didn't. She had buried her grief by busying herself with school and Noah, but her grief refused to be forgotten. She'd barely made it through the fall semester. Early into the spring, her control had vaporized. Numbly, she walked through the days, making lame excuses to her students and her advisor that just sounded pathetic. A bright and capable person should have been able to manage. She hadn't.

Dr. Lamanski was right. This was an extraordinary opportunity to jumpstart her project, but it would cost her. Besides airfare, she would need living expenses. With no work visa, she wouldn't be able to work there. Olivia needed to think. "I'll let you know tomorrow."

Her advisor nodded. "ASAP."

On the drive home, Olivia weighed her options. The alternative to going to Scotland was staying home and substitute teaching to replace the assistantship income she'd lost. Other than airfare and living expenses, everything else was the same. But then she remembered one thing that would be different. If she stayed home, she would have to pay rent. Scotland was rent free. She reviewed her account containing the life insurance benefit and small inheritance her mother had left her. It had been so unexpected that she'd put it in an investment account and left it. She looked at the balance. She had no school debt due thanks to going to a state school on scholarship and commuting from home for her undergraduate work. Her graduate assistantship had covered tuition, but that was gone now. She was on a month-to-month lease, so she could either sublet her apartment or give notice and move everything into a storage unit. If she dipped into her trust for airfare, tuition, and living expenses, she could manage. She stared at the numbers. Yes, she could manage!

Two weeks later, she boarded a flight bound for Scotland.

3

Now warm and dry in the charming Edinburgh pub, Olivia relaxed. For the first time since her whirlwind trip to Scotland, a sense of contentment settled upon her. It wasn't just the comforting shelter from a damp Scottish day. It was Edinburgh itself. Rain and all, she loved it. Wherever she looked, history gazed back from red sandstone buildings, prompting her to wonder about the stories they had to tell. Some of those stories of Scotland existed in song. She couldn't wait to hear them in person. She'd heard them in her mind as she read them from sheet music, and she'd heard dozens of recordings. Now, she was here in the land and immersed in the culture they had emerged from. She was in Scotland!

A weight she hadn't known she was carrying lifted from her shoulders. She had made the right move. Her mind raced with plans and ideas. Not only could she work free of distractions, but here, at the source of the stories and songs, she would hear them in the same pubs they'd been sung in for centuries. There were places to visit—the Highlands, of course. But first, she would get her bearings and explore Edinburgh.

She caught herself smiling and practically laughed at the thought of how she must look, smiling to herself all alone. At least she wasn't talking to herself. Yet. After a semester alone with no one to talk to, she might get to that point.

Her phone rang. It was Noah. *You're the one who missed having someone to talk to.*

While making her travel preparations, Olivia had set aside thoughts of Noah's disgruntled reaction. But now, in the pub, as she stared at her phone, the memory of their last conversation rushed to the surface. It hadn't gone well.

She considered ignoring his call, but that didn't feel right. Neither did taking his call in public. It could get emotional. But the phone kept ringing, so she took a breath and answered. "Hello." Her voice didn't sound as cheerful as she'd meant for it to.

Noah didn't seem to notice. "I'm on a lunch break. I timed it to coincide with the end of your workday."

"Oh." *Good. That sounds more upbeat.* Noah didn't sound awkward at all, which was odd, since they'd just broken up—or agreed on a break.

THE BREAK HAD BEEN his idea, but she didn't put up a fight. She wasn't the sort to cling to a guy who didn't want her, so she'd agreed to the break. She rolled her eyes. *A break?*

It was a breakup. Calling it anything else was a cowardly way to ease through the transition. Olivia was more of a rip-the-Band-Aid-off sort, but preferring to focus on trip preparations, she'd avoided the issue and went along with the fiction of an interim break.

The Scotland trip broke something between them. Until then, their biggest decisions had involved choosing a restaurant for dinner or weekend brunch. Looking back, she could see it was part of what made their relationship work. With no pressing choices to make, they just did things together with no friction between them. So when Scotland came up, Olivia hadn't thought Noah would mind. Of course he would miss her, just like she would miss him. If a relationship couldn't survive a semester apart, its foundation wasn't strong enough. She didn't like it, but the facts were the facts. Her career was at stake. She didn't have a choice. While a semester in Scotland was a big change, it would not affect Noah except for the free time he would have without her around.

Noah didn't see it that way. He didn't want her to go. He was adamant about it. He seemed to believe Olivia would change her mind and stay home—not for their relationship but for his convenience. He hadn't bothered to factor in what was best for Olivia. Noah's wishes always won out over Olivia's struggles.

For days, they'd discussed, argued, and analyzed it, but Olivia saw no other way. The day before her flight, Noah had issued a final ultimatum. "If you go to Scotland, it's over."

Surrounded by stacks of clothing and travel gear, she'd looked up from her packing list and quietly said, "Okay." She was done. She was going to Scotland.

After a long moment of slack-jawed disbelief, Noah had left.

As breakups went, theirs was a clean one. He'd called back later that evening and rebranded it as a break. Olivia had let him. He could call it whatever he wanted. She was tired of talking. She'd even listened as he suggested the separation would give them perspective. They might even be stronger when she returned home. By that point, all she heard were words—empty words. It was over, and she was relieved. That surprised her.

Noah must have gone home and realized he might not find someone better while she was gone. She imagined him making a contingency flowchart. If he met someone, fine. If no one better came along, he would keep Olivia as a backup. She tried, but she couldn't find a more positive way to view it. Noah always examined every angle to determine the best option—for him. She didn't doubt that served him well in his job, but Olivia wasn't a work issue. She was the woman he cared for— or used to care for. But she couldn't get past wondering how much he could have cared if his knee-jerk reaction was to dump her. She would never have done that to him.

That was when she'd known it was over. She could breathe. She couldn't call herself happy about it—not yet—but it was for the best. In Edinburgh, she felt more centered than she had in months. She had made the right move. She would soak in the culture and finish her project without Noah to distract her.

Except here he was on her phone, going on about work as if nothing had happened, while she sat in a pub with an ocean between them. He prattled on for a minute or two then launched into his reason for calling.

"I'm still trying to understand the timing of your Highland vacation."

She shut her eyes for a moment. "Well... it's not a vacation, and Edinburgh isn't the Highlands."

"Whatever. I miss you. Come home. You can finish studying here."

"Studying?" *It's not a pop quiz I can cram for. It's my dissertation. My career!*

"Don't worry about your apartment sublet. Stay here. You won't have to pay rent, and I'll help you! I'll bring you coffee in the mornings and dinner at night. You won't have to do anything except schoolwork."

She glanced up as Max appeared and took her empty soup bowl. She lowered her voice. "That's what I'm doing here."

Max returned to the bar.

Noah said, "There are planes leaving daily."

"But I won't be on one, because I'm not coming home."

In the periphery, she caught a sideways glance from Max. *Did I say that too loudly?*

Noah asked, "Don't you think you're being a little selfish?"

"Don't *you*?" She snapped back without thinking, which didn't do either of them any good. "Look, let's not argue. Let's stick with the plan."

"Oh, right, the plan." She had never heard Noah sound so sarcastic. "You mean the break? Are you sure that's what you want?"

"It was your idea."

"Yes. And you agreed."

"Right." In the long silence that followed, Olivia

brushed some stray blond wisps of hair from her face and glanced about, searching for words. Without intending to, she locked eyes with Max, who was pulling a draft. He must've seen something in her expression, because he narrowed his eyes. It could have been a look of concern... or annoyance. She wondered which then dismissed the thought. She couldn't think of that now, not while Noah was still on the phone. He was rehashing the same issues that had prompted their so-called break while Olivia shifted her position and stared at the fire in the wood stove.

When he seemed to have finished, she said, "I get what you're saying. You think I've made a mistake. But I don't, and I'm here. My work's going well, and I'm not coming home."

"I don't like it."

Olivia frowned. "I know, and I'm sorry you feel that way."

He said nothing.

When she couldn't take any more silence, she said, "I've got to go."

He muttered a quiet and miserable "Bye."

Olivia lowered her head and rubbed her forehead with her fingertips, drawing in a deep breath. She exhaled, and when she straightened up, Max was beside her. *How does he do that—just appear out of nowhere?*

"Sorry. I didn't mean to startle you." He set down a half-pint of beer.

She glanced up with a questioning look.

"I poured the wrong beer for someone, and I didn't want to waste it. It's your brand, so..." Before she could protest, he returned to the bar.

Olivia sipped her beer and soaked in her surroundings. The after-work crowd had thinned out, and the pub had grown quiet. Only the dull murmur of patrons seated at the bar and a few scattered tables interrupted the soothing crackle of the fire.

By the time she had emptied her glass, she'd arrived at a conclusion. The Noah plan wasn't working. With the prospect of angsty phone calls looming on the horizon, she didn't want the drama. It was time to turn Noah's break into a breakup.

She pulled out her phone and drafted a text. "Noah, I'm sorry. I know this whole thing has upset you. But I need to do this. It's not fair for me to ask you to accept it. You deserve better, and I deserve..." She backspaced. "We both need some space." *No, not space. That sounds too temporary.* She deleted the last bit. "We both need to move on. Goodbye, Noah."

She paused. *Are you really going to break up in a text? Coward! Call him and break up over the phone!* She stared at her phone and deleted the text.

It was five hours earlier in New York. Despite dreading having to make the call, she wanted to get it over with. But she couldn't call him now. His lunchtime was over, and he would be back at work. She could call him that night.

When she'd finished her beer, she shoved her phone into her satchel. The zipper was stuck. *Come on!* As she wrestled with it, her frustration with Noah came to the surface. She yanked the tab back and forth. *Dang it, this thing will not close!* She couldn't just walk home with it open. Something might fall out—or worse, someone could pick her pocket. She gave the zipper one last exasperated yank and set the bag down on the table, which was better than her first impulse—hurling it to the floor.

She blew air through her lips. *Calm down and think. It's a five-minute walk. Hold it close. You'll be fine. Or you could try it again.* She took a few cleansing breaths and gave the zipper a pull. It was hopeless. She let out an exasperated sound.

A shadow crossed over the table. She lifted her eyes to find Max setting down an armload of wood for the fire.

He stood, with a touch of pity and a glint of amusement in his eyes. "Need some help?"

If the aggravation hadn't brought enough color to her face, now she was embarrassed, and that made it worse. He held out his hand.

She frowned and slid the bag across the table toward him. "Good luck."

Olivia watched skeptically as he tried it and failed. Only his blue eyes and Scottish charm kept her from saying, "I told you so."

He examined the zipper for a few moments then pulled a golf pencil from his pocket and rubbed it over the zipper teeth. He pulled the tab back and forth for a couple of seconds. Like magic, it opened, and he set it back down on the table.

She was stunned. "How did you do that?"

"It's a gift."

She didn't mean to frown.

He smirked and lifted the pencil. "It's the graphite. It's a lubricant."

Olivia didn't understand, but before she could ask, he interrupted her thoughts. "So you're American."

It was an odd segue, but she was happy enough to move on from zippers and lubricants. She nodded.

"From...?"

"New York. Upstate, not the city." Silent smiles followed, so she added, "And you're Scottish? Just a guess."

She liked the way his eyes lit up when he grinned. It was infectious. But these awkward silences were getting to her.

"Very perceptive."

She shrugged. "It's a gift."

His eyes met hers. It was then that Olivia first realized there was something special between them. He must have felt it too—a spark of attraction that made them both pause, surprised by its sudden intensity.

Olivia wasn't exactly inexperienced with men. Before Noah, she'd dated and had a couple of somewhat-serious and almost-long-term relationships, depending on how one defined *long-term*. But she'd never felt so exhilarated yet terrified as she did at that moment. It was like being struck by lightning in the instant before pain from the burns settled in. The pub she'd found so cozy now seemed to close in on her. She averted her eyes, only to feel his gaze more acutely. There was only one thing to do—escape!

Olivia stood, but while trying to avoid brushing against him, she lost her balance and faltered. Max took hold of her elbow long enough to steady her, then he let go. The fact that he looked as stunned as she felt didn't help.

"Thanks." She slung her satchel over her shoulder then glanced at his twinkling eyes. Big mistake. He was so close, she could smell him. And it wasn't grocery aisle seven. She caught a whiff of beer, which was an occupational hazard, so she couldn't fault him for that. His shirt smelled freshly laundered. Her heart pounded. That was some powerful laundry detergent they sold over here.

She sidled past him and walked to the exit, rejoicing that her knees hadn't buckled. She nearly collided with an incoming couple at the doorway. With a breathless "Excuse me," she made it outside and hurried along the sidewalk until she could round the corner and catch her breath.

4

M ax stared at the empty doorway. That American woman had issues. If the pub hadn't been so busy, he might have taken a moment or two to find out what they were. That was all it took to satisfy his curiosity, usually.

An exaggerated female sigh interrupted his thoughts. "Pretty? Check. Blond? Check. Max's rapt attention? Check."

He turned toward the familiar voice to catch a broad grin blooming on his coworker's face.

"Did you ask her out? No. Because... Why?"

He returned a stony expression. "There's a couple at the end of the bar that look thirsty."

With a shrug, she headed down to the end of the bar.

Once again, Max had avoided Esme's misguided efforts to fix him, but he knew she would try again. It didn't matter that he didn't need fixing when she thought he did.

Esme knew him too well. In their first year at university, he and Esme had been in some classes together. When her finances forced her to drop out of school, she came looking for work at the pub. She didn't want to go home to her family's small farm in the lowlands. She loved her life in the city too much, so Max took pity on her and gave her a job. Though it'd started as a favor, she'd proven herself with hard work. Seven years later, he doubted he could run the place without her. He paid her enough to avoid finding out.

When all the patrons' glasses were full and the emptied ones washed, Esme dried her hands on a bar towel and said, "She's your type."

"Who?"

She gave him a knowing look.

"I don't have a type." He looked away, wishing it were a busier Tuesday.

"Yes, you do!"

Max folded his arms and nearly asked how she could possibly know. But he knew he didn't want to hear the answer.

"You get a look on your face."

"Aye, right." He turned to walk away, but she continued. He made the mistake of pausing and turning.

"Your eyes get glassy, and your mouth goes slack—just a wee bit—like you've been hit by a tranquilizer dart. You don't even squirm. You just lie there and drool." She leaned forward and winked. "Ladies love a man with a bit of drool on his chin."

He hid his amusement. It would only encourage her.

She assumed a dramatic pose and continued. "And you stare like you're gazing into a Scots mist. It's the same look you get when you cannae find your car in the car park."

"You've never seen me look for my car in a car park."

She leveled a wry look at him. "I don't have to 'cause I ken how you'd look—like you do when an attractive blonde walks into the pub." She appeared struck by a revelation. "Come to think of it, that American was attractive and blond. Hmm... It's almost as if you have a type."

"It's almost as if you don't know what you were talking about." But she did. Max just refused to admit it.

Esme folded her arms and leaned back against the bar. "In our global connections class, it was the girl in the front row with the straight, shoulder-length ponytail."

"What? You're delusional."

Ignoring his protests, she went on. "I remember it well. It was so entertaining to watch you watch her and her unnaturally yellow hair. She just swished it around like a pretty pony on parade."

He couldn't disagree.

"Then the next semester, it was the English Lit girl." She squinted. "That was a bit of a stretch because her hair was more on the dark side of blond. Wasn't it? You could even call it light brown. I guess you made an exception."

He surrendered with a shrug. "It was English Lit, and I love a literate mind." Her mind wasn't the only thing he'd loved about her. He took a moment to recall how much he'd enjoyed that view.

Esme pointed at him. "There it is!"

"There what is?"

"The look! Glistening eyes, and your mouth kind of turns up on the side—like you're on the verge of a smile."

Max's face flushed as he scoffed, "You're off your head!" He scowled, but the look on Esme's face made him laugh.

She touched her chin. "Let's see... The next one was..." Her expression went blank. "Oh."

The next one was Paulina. Esme looked guilty. "Sorry."

Max shook his head. "No, please go on. Tell me all about Paulina—the woman who ripped out my heart, stomped on it, then ground it into the cobbled street with her bootheel before boarding the next train to London."

Unwilling to face Esme's remorse—or worse, pity—Max set about tidying the bar.

PAULINA. She was his first love, the kind that carves a glacial-scale wound to the heart and leaves a gnarled scar when it's over.

When he had to drop out of school, they'd stayed together. She would stop by the pub after class, sit by the fire—in the same seat where the American had sat—and study. But in time, Paulina grew busy. They spent less and less time together until, by her fourth year of university, she spent more time with her friends than with him. Looking back, Max realized their last year together was a drawn-out process of drifting apart.

When Paulina got into the London School of Economics, she wanted to make a clean break, but they couldn't seem to let go. After all, they were only a train ride away. They could manage. So she moved to London. A month later, on a video call, she said, "It's not working, is it?"

It hadn't been, but he hadn't been ready to give up. Before he could speak, a door opened, and a male voice called out, "Paula? Come here, hen!" No one ever called her Paula. Or hen. Her wide-eyed, stunned expression said it all. The screen went blank.

A few minutes later, she called back, this time without video. "I'm sorry. I didn't mean for you to find out like that. I'm sorry."

He heard himself mutter, "Right. Well, I've got to go." And he hung up.

A few months later, she called, crying. Her new guy had left her. She missed Max. She was sorry, and he believed her. He forgave her but ended it—for good this time.

That was the last time they spoke. He heard she'd finished school and gotten a job in a think tank. She was on track to accomplish everything she'd hoped to achieve. *Good for her.* He meant it. Maybe things could have been different if he'd stayed in school. But he was here. She was there. End of story.

WHEN THE LAST customers had walked out the door, Esme went over to Max. "I'm an eejit."

"Aye." He smiled.

She looked relieved. "Ask her out."

Max pointed at the couple paused in the doorway to embrace. "I would, but she looks kind of busy at the moment."

"Not her! The American. She's perfect for you."

Max rolled his eyes. "And how would you know?"

"Well, she's pretty. And she's smart. She's a little quiet, but you're not a big talker."

"And you know all about her because...?"

Esme shrugged. "She left her satchel unzipped, so I did the maths. Computer plus notebook equals student. Ergo, smart."

Max wrinkled his face. "In theory."

"Which makes her perfect for you."

Max shook his head. "No more students, especially an American student!"

"Why not?"

Max couldn't believe what he was hearing. "Remember Paulina and London? New York's even farther."

"New York? Did you read her passport while you were digging through her bag?"

"I didn't dig through her bag. I fixed her zipper."

Esme raised an eyebrow. "Handy with zippers, are you?"

Ignoring her, he continued. "And she happened to mention it."

Esme narrowed her eyes. "Oh, did she? She didn't share that with me. She must enjoy talking to you."

Max drew in a breath and exhaled. "She was being polite."

Esme's face lit up. "I could visit you in New York! That would be brilliant!"

"And impossible." It was time to burst Esme's bubble. "Even if we fell madly in love—which we won't—"

"Why not?"

"Because. Besides, this pub has been in my family for generations. I quit school so we could keep it in the family, so I'm not packing up and moving to New York or anywhere else."

"You could hire a manager."

"My parents would love that." He peered at her through narrowed eyes. "You know what you need? A hobby."

Esme heaved a sigh. "It's the twenty-first century. We've got Zoom and Skype."

"But you can't pull a pint through a screen. Have you ever tried knitting?"

Esme's eyes brightened. "Wait. You don't know that she still lives there. She might have moved here."

Max considered the possibility then scoffed. "Are you sure you're not the one with the crush?" He cringed inwardly. *Did I just admit to having a crush?*

Esme fired back. "Not my type. But you know whose type she is? Yours."

"This is ridiculous. She came in to get out of the rain."

Esme raised an eyebrow. "It's meant to be—and we'll know it the next time it rains."

Max looked at his watch. "Which should be any minute."

Esme smiled knowingly. "Trust me. She'll be back."

Max rolled his eyes. "Your imagination is astounding."

"Not imagination—second sight."

"You've got second sight? I've got second thoughts."

Esme pouted. "What do you have against true love?"

"That's not what this is."

"How can you be sure if you won't give it a chance?"

"Oh, I'm sure... that you need a hobby."

"Like matchmaking?"

"No!"

"Why not?"

"Because you're terrible at it!"

Esme glared. "Well, that's just misinformation!"

Max rubbed his forehead. Much to his relief, Esme disappeared through the kitchen door, but she returned moments later with a rack of clean glasses. As she passed by, she muttered, "She'll be back."

"Unless she's on holiday and leaving tomorrow."

"On holiday, with a satchel?"

Max shrugged. "Or here for business. Regardless, she'll go home at some point, so you can stop planning the wedding."

Esme's shoulders slumped. "I didn't say to marry her. Just take her out."

Max didn't bother to respond. He had made himself clear enough.

Esme persisted. "Just because things didn't work out in the past doesn't mean they can't in the future. It's like they say. If you fall off a horse..."

"You should tell the person you're with—and their horse—to leave you alone."

Esme looked patiently at him. "That is not what they say."

That's it. Time to shut this down. He hated to do it, but there was no other way. He looked straight into Esme's eyes. "And what about your type?"

Esme flinched. "That's different."

Bull's-eye. Max knew she had feelings for someone, but she wouldn't tell him who. It seemed clear that her feelings weren't returned. From the hint of pain in her eyes at the moment, Max feared his point had landed too hard. He said gently, "Maybe we're both better off as we are."

Esme rallied, as she always did. She was tough, so tough that the regulars knew not to mess with her. Anyone who did soon found themselves at the receiving end of her sharp wit—and sometimes her sharp tongue. Esme shifted the focus right back to Max. "She likes you."

Max rolled his eyes. "Oh, aye. So we're back on this, are we?"

She nodded. "For starters, she watched you walk away."

He balked. "So watching me walk away means she loves me—or she wants to order another pint."

"She likes you."

"Brilliant theory."

"I wouldn't call it a theory exactly. I just know if a woman watches a man walk away, she's either admiring the view or there's toilet paper trailing out of his trousers. Wait, turn around. Let me check you for toilet paper."

Max swatted her hands away before she could grasp hold of his shoulders. "You're the annoying sister I never had!" He walked into the kitchen.

She called after him. "Because I'm looking out for you! And you're lucky to have me!"

He leaned on the fridge but stopped short of hitting his head against it.

Esme leaned against the doorframe and folded her arms. "Are you praying for her to come back?"

"I wasn't praying, but if it'll get your mind off this, I'm willing to try it! Until then, who's minding the bar?"

With a mischievous twinkle in her eyes, Esme walked back through the swinging doors.

Max stayed in the kitchen to clean up, if for no other reason than to avoid Esme's fixation on his nonexistent love life.

He would never admit to Esme that she was right about the American. He did have a type, and she was indeed it. They'd had something—a connection or chemistry... He shook his head. And she'd taken a phone call, probably from someone at home.

No doubt her husband, you numpty!

Hours later, Esme left, and Max locked the door and headed up the back stairs that led to his apartment. Once there, he sank into his favorite overstuffed chair and turned on the TV. He stared without listening. It was Esme's fault the American was still on his mind.

It wasn't like he hadn't dated. He'd gone out with several women. Esme had left that part out—probably because he seldom got past a third date. Not that he didn't want a relationship; he just didn't want the ones he'd had so far.

Above all, he didn't want a relationship with

another ambitious career woman, especially not an American from New York who, in all likelihood, would leave him.

No, that is not gonnae happen! He drew in a satisfied breath and exhaled. *Well, that's sorted.*

He leaned forward, elbows on knees, and refocused on the football match he'd been trying to watch. "Not gonnae happen."

5

Olivia stopped at the Sainsbury's local convenience store to grab some essentials then headed up to her flat. Its entrance opened to a long hallway leading to a great room with a kitchen on one side. On the opposite side, a wall of windows offered a stunning view of the Meadows, a grassy expanse criss-crossed by tree-canopied walkways. Her modern glass building towered over historic stone buildings lining the Meadows. There, individuals often sat reading while others pushed strollers. In the afternoon, teams assembled to play soccer, or as they called it, football. Their distant voices wafted into the air, along with the occasional grinding of skateboard wheels on the sidewalks.

The location was ideal, with the library and museum a short walk away and Old Town a few minutes farther. She could go everywhere she wanted on foot. Inside, the apartment was modern and tastefully furnished in warm, neutral earth tones, lending it a tranquil atmosphere that was enhanced by the view.

By the time she'd finished unpacking her shopping

bag and tucked it away in her satchel, the teakettle was steaming. On her rainy walk home, she'd decided hot chocolate would make everything better. While stirring the contents of her cup, she looked through the window. A hovering mist in the twilight cast an otherworldly glow on the Scottish hills in the distance. Even there, Noah found an unwelcome way into her thoughts. It was more of a habit, which she needed to break.

Noah had never been a soulmate, but at some point in their journey together, she'd decided she'd outgrown the concept. All those childish notions of love at first sight and the passion she saw in the movies were fine to imagine, but this was real life. She had something even better—a companionable man who had the usual qualities that appealed to most women. He was pleasant looking, and he strove to do all the right things, like bring her chocolate and flowers on special days like her birthday. Noah was dutiful and thoughtful, and he treated her well. The only drama they shared was in choosing the TV shows and movies they watched together. Above all, Noah was consistent—until he'd broken up with her.

At midnight, which would be Noah's dinnertime back home, Olivia picked up her phone and called him. It went to voicemail. *Great.* She was doing the math to determine the best time to catch him the next morning when her phone rang.

"Noah, hi."

"Hi, Livy."

She'd never liked Noah's nickname for her, but he

seemed to enjoy having his own little term of endearment for her, so she overlooked it.

He said, "It's good to hear your voice."

"Yeah." It was. Talking to him took her back to a time before Scotland, when everything felt comfortable. But now, she couldn't find the words to begin.

"So... how's Scotland?"

"Good. Great, really. I love it."

More silence followed, then she said, "I've just been to a pub. It's charming. It's got live music most evenings, so I'll have to go back soon."

"I hope you had your umbrella."

"What?" She hadn't expected the concern.

"The weather report said it was going to rain."

She blinked slowly. That was so Noah, checking the weather for her. "No, actually, I forgot it. But I had my raincoat, so... happy ending."

"Could you take the sticker off your phone lens?"

She froze for a moment. "No, I'm... I can't at the moment." Guilt churned in her stomach. What she had to say would go over better without facial expressions. The long pause wasn't helping, so she forged ahead. "Is this a good time?"

He replied in his usual practical tone. "I wouldn't have called you back if it weren't."

Olivia caught herself frowning. At least Noah couldn't see it. "I know, but... I mean, is it a good time to talk?"

He paused long enough for Olivia to feel uncomfortable. "Of course."

While Olivia searched for the right words, Noah asked, "How's Scotland?"

He'd asked about that and the weather. "It's good."

"Good."

It's your turn. Say something, like "It's over. It's no longer a break. We're officially broken." That would get the job done, but she couldn't be so blunt. Or she could say, "Let's just stop pretending. We both know it's over." *No, that's just a wordier version of blunt.* As the silence grew unbearable, she simply started talking with no aim in sight, hoping the right words would come. She drew in a breath.

Noah blurted, "I miss you."

Well, that didn't help. There were certain statements meant to be echoed back, like expressions of affection and maybe the weather. But Olivia couldn't voice the words. In her own way, she did miss him or how they used to be. But that couple was gone, and they weren't coming back. *Just say it.* "The reason I called—" *The reason you called? You sound like you're confirming a dental appointment.* "I've been thinking."

"Me too."

Olivia drew in a deep breath. "I think we should—"

"Get married."

"—break up." *Married?* She blinked. "What?" She'd heard him, but something inside disconnected the meaning.

"Nothing."

He'd said it so quickly, while she was still talking, that she wasn't sure she'd heard him correctly. *Get married? Did he say get married?* It was so quiet, Olivia wondered if the call had dropped. "Noah?"

He laughed. It was awkward and forced. His voice brightened. "Haha! We could go to that casino upstate. Do they have Elvis impersonators, or is that just in Vegas? I'm kidding. What do they do there in Scotland?

Get married by Elvis in a kilt? We should do that so I can start calling you Sasquatch."

"Sassenach."

"Or Sassy for short."

Is he serious? No. Maybe. "I think there's a tradition of going to Gretna Green to get married by a blacksmith." She was just saying words now, to distract from the awkwardness.

"You're kidding. A blacksmith? So, like Elvis with an anvil?"

Olivia winced. "Uh... no, not really."

"Oh, so just Elvis in a kilt? It would have to be young Elvis. A kilt wouldn't look right over that white jumpsuit, would it?"

"I don't know. Noah, I think—"

He interrupted. "I'd like to hear 'Hound Dog' on the bagpipes."

"I wouldn't! Noah—" Suddenly aware she was practically shouting, Olivia lowered her voice. "Noah, I'm sorry. I think we should break up. I mean really break up—make it final."

His voice faltered halfway through, but he got the words out. "Break up? Just like that?"

"Otherwise, we'd just be postponing the inevitable."

"Yeah, I guess..."

"I'm sorry."

He cleared his throat. "Well, I've got a busy day tomorrow, so..."

The pain in his voice wasn't easy to hear, but she pressed on. "It's for the best, don't you think?"

He didn't answer.

She imagined him weeping or being too angry to

speak. Or maybe there was nothing left to say. "Well... take care of yourself."

He cleared his throat. "Yeah."

"No hard feelings?" *Of course there are hard feelings! Stop talking. You're making it worse.*

The third act of Puccini's "La Boheme" started playing in her head. *Addio, senza rancor.* The curse of having been a voice major was that every dramatic event had a corresponding musical reference. In this case, it was two angsty Parisian Bohemians breaking up in the snow. *Goodbye without rancor.* At least she hadn't said that—or worse, sung it—in Italian. Noah would have cringed. As much as he loved going out, attending an opera was a line he wouldn't cross.

At least she and Noah were breaking up better than the Bohemians. They caved in and stayed together until the spring. That poor girl wanted out so badly, she coughed herself to death. That was why a clean break was the best way to go.

Noah interrupted her thoughts. "Goodbye, Livy."

"Bye, Noah." *Addio.*

She ended the call and stared at her phone. *That was miserable.* No wonder composers wrote songs about it. Puccini and Sedaka were right. Breaking up *was* hard to do.

She stared into the distance. "But I did it! It's over!" She exhaled, and an unexpected wave of relief washed over her. Then a sobering thought came to mind. *Did he really propose? Nah. He was being sarcastic. Wasn't he? He must have been. He was the one who wanted to break up first. Yeah, he was kidding. He laughed. Sort of.*

Guilt churned in her stomach. *I hope he's okay.* She stared out the window at the hills in the distance.

Because I feel okay. No, I'm better than that. New guilt tried to grip her, but she drew in a deep, cleansing breath and exhaled.

THE RED ROSE was on her way to all the places she tended to go, so she passed it every day that week. Aside from a fleeting glance as she passed it, she walked on and focused on her work goals for the day. A morning at the library left her wanting a change of scenery, so she headed through Old Town and on down to Princes Street.

After a two-hour detour at the Scottish National Gallery, she headed across the street to Waterstones. She'd read its second-floor coffee shop overlooked Princes Street. It did not disappoint. Three hours and four tables later, she'd worked her way to a prime spot by the window. Below, an endless stream of pedestrians, buses, and trams passed. Swept into a productive writing frenzy by the view and her favorite playlist, she worked until closing. As a sales associate waited, Olivia typed a few hasty notes to help her pick up where she'd left off, then she packed up her computer and left.

Outside, she fell into pace with the busy rush-hour foot traffic and headed for home. It was then she remembered it was Friday. Her plan was to spend every Friday and Saturday night—and more if she could—listening to live traditional folk music in pubs. But first, she would stop home and unload her backpack.

After freshening up, she headed back out. As she neared The Red Rose, a young woman with a violin backpack case entered the pub. Close behind, a man with a guitar slung over his shoulder followed. She'd intended to try someplace new, but The Red Rose was so close to home, it made a perfect first stop for her traditional Scottish music experience.

The pub bustled with people. Lively music filled the air, but it wasn't until she worked her way to the back that she saw the musicians all seated around a couple of tables. There was a fiddle, a guitar, Scottish smallpipes, an acoustic bass, and a tin whistle. The sound filled her with joy. The recordings and videos she'd studied couldn't compare to the experience of being in a Scottish pub as live musicians jammed traditional folk music. There was no place to sit, so she found a pillar to lean on. They finished a jig, took swigs of beer, and started a strathspey. From a nearby table, three young women got up and began to step dance. This was what she'd come to Scotland for. She was experiencing a tradition that had gone on for generations. It was more than hearing musicians at the top of their game. Some were, but the musical skill level varied. That was part of the tradition that went beyond music to a sense of community. Being there made Olivia part of it.

A pint of dark beer appeared before her. She turned to find the female bartender. Olivia had been so engrossed in the music, she hadn't thought to go to the bar for a drink. "Oh, thanks! Hold on." She dug into her pocket for cash, but the bartender waved her off and walked away. Olivia looked past her. Without thinking, she scanned the bar for Max, but all she saw was a young male bartender she hadn't seen before.

Look at you, rebound girl. How long has it been since you broke up with Noah? Five minutes? Oh, right, a few days. Yeah. You do not need a boyfriend. Was that what she was doing—looking for a boyfriend? That wasn't what she wanted. Sure, the guy was attractive, but a lot of guys were attractive. That meant nothing.

You're here for the music, which is amazing. So pay attention. Besides, he was nowhere to be found. She was relieved about that. A relationship—or even a date—was the last thing she needed. That distraction would throw her work out of focus and, at worst, derail it. She could not let that happen again. She would not.

But there was nothing wrong with enjoying the scenery. No one could dispute what a beautiful country it was. What better way to appreciate it than total cultural immersion. Her work would be better if she were to flesh out the context. She nodded. *That's all I'm doing—just fleshing out the context.*

The musicians took a break, and the pub quieted down a notch. Olivia steeled her resolve. *You're here to research, and you're doing a fantastic job. Just stay focused.*

"Have you changed your mind about dark beer?"

She recognized Max's voice before she looked up—which meant nothing. She was, after all, a musician. It was perfectly natural to home in on his resonant baritone timbre. That didn't explain losing herself in his gaze, though.

"You're not drinking your beer."

Olivia looked down at the beer as if she hadn't known it was there, then she came to her senses. "Oh, I will. I was just thinking." *Please don't ask about what.* She raised her glass slightly. "But thanks for this."

Now it was his turn to look confused.

Olivia peered at him. "The beer. Thanks."

Understanding dawned on his face. "That must be Esme's doing."

"Pardon?"

"Esme, my coworker. She gave that to you."

It felt like a question, so she answered him. "Oh." *Was I not meant to have it?* "I must have misunderstood. No problem. I can pay for it." She reached for her purse, but he touched her wrist.

"You will not! At least not for this one."

Olivia looked at his hand, still on her wrist, then looked up at him.

His eyes lost their sparkle, and he withdrew his hand. "Well... cheers."

She stared at his back as he walked away. *What just happened?*

An outburst of laughter rang out from the door, where a dozen more people had squeezed into the pub. She might have noticed them before if her attention hadn't been drawn elsewhere. While the musicians returned from a break and picked up their instruments, Olivia tried to figure out why she felt... however she felt. That was the problem. She didn't know what she felt, except different. She wasn't herself. Maybe it was Scotland. Everything seemed so misty and magical here. It was a romantic explanation, but she preferred it to the more mundane truth. Breakups made people go temporarily mad. This rebound situation was distorting her perception of Scotland and Max, except Scotland truly was magical. *And Max?* She stole a glance, as if she needed confirmation. Yes, Max was still more attractive than a man ought to be.

With that decided, Olivia turned her attention to the music's six-eight meter, driven by the bodhrán's steady ostinato and a lively fiddle melody. All of Olivia's distractions gave way to joy as she took in the sound and the sight of musicians looking not so unlike those from past generations. She could almost envision the progression of these same songs and instruments through the years. The instruments may have evolved, and the harmonic progressions might stray from their simpler origins, but the essence of the songs was unchanged. If any ghosts of past musicians eavesdropped, they would approve.

A sudden cold sensation shocked her, as if one of the Greyfriars Kirkyard apparitions had wandered off the campus and drifted through her. But it wasn't a ghost—unless ghosts smelled like beer. A guy standing nearby had gestured too broadly and struck the guy beside him, whose beer had just poured down her favorite white top. Stunned, she froze until the guy who'd spilled the beer pulled off his T-shirt and started blotting her chest, all the while slurring an unintelligible series of apologies.

Olivia swatted his hands away. "Thank you. I'm fine. Really. It's okay."

It wasn't. *She* wasn't—especially when she followed several gazes and glanced down to find her chest oversharing through her wet blouse.

She was turning to leave when Max appeared and ushered her into the kitchen.

"What are you doing?" she asked, clutching her arms around herself.

"I can't let you go home like that."

"I don't need your permission."

"No, you don't. But you need this." He unbuttoned and whipped off his shirt. That looked a little heroic.

And he wasn't even the first guy tonight to pull off his shirt for her. Scotland *was* magical! If she had any doubts, the remaining black T-shirt that clung to Max's well-defined muscles drove the point home.

Looking anywhere but at Olivia, Max thrust his shirt at her. "Put this on."

With a thank-you, she put it on and returned to the pub, followed closely by Max. As the beer spiller's friend guided him to the door, Olivia hesitated and turned to Max. "I think I'll give him a head start."

"How far do you have to go?"

"It's just a five-minute walk."

Without hesitating, he said, "I'll walk you home."

"Thanks, but I'll be fine. I'll bring the shirt back tomorrow."

As she headed for the door, she heard Max say, "No rush!"

6

The next morning, Max pulled the last chair from a tabletop and set it down on the floor.

Looking slightly disheveled, Esme dashed in with a bottle of Irn-Bru in her hand. "Sorry I'm late."

"Are you?" Max glanced at his watch and dismissed it with a shrug. "Two minutes."

She got to work behind the bar while Max sat at the bar and placed some supply orders online. He closed the lid on his laptop. "So, what are you doing?"

"Restocking the bar," she replied nonchalantly without looking up.

"That's not what I meant."

She stopped what she was doing and peered at him. "Do you mean what am I doing for the rest of my life? Or what am I doing with an extensive knowledge of comparative literature, wiping sloshed beer from a bar top?"

He was about to explain that her gift of a half-pint to the American hadn't escaped him. She was up to something, but the door rattled before he could speak.

"We're closed! Oh!"

Olivia stood outside the locked door, but she left before he could reach it.

"I don't think she saw me."

Esme said wryly, "My God, you're perceptive."

He fumbled frantically with the lock then rushed outside. He would hear about that from Esme, but he could deal with her later. "Wait! Miss!"

She turned and smiled.

Dazzled by her smile and relieved to have caught her, he stared for a moment then came to his senses. "Was that you at the door?" *Of course it was, genius.*

"Yeah, I was just passing by, and I wanted to thank you." She reached into a large tote bag. "And return this." They ended up face-to-face a few doors down from the pub. "It might be a little damp. The washer-dryer combo was tricky."

He couldn't decide whether her hair was honey blond or golden. Esme was right. He did have a type! At least Esme couldn't see him now. *Unless...* He turned back to find Esme outside, arms folded as she leaned her shoulder on the outside wall, wearing a knowing expression. *Great.*

As Olivia handed over the shirt, her cheeks flushed with color. "This was nice of you. Thanks."

Max shrugged and shook his head, all the while feeling awkward. "So... off to work?"

She smiled and looked more at ease. "Yeah. Duty calls." She nodded and glanced down the street.

"Where do you work?"

"Wherever I want to, really."

A list of occupations ran through his head as he tried to imagine what she meant. Before he could ask, she said, "I'm finishing—or rather, trying to finish my dissertation." She paused. "It's a... long paper I have to do for a doctorate."

"I know what a dissertation is."

Her face went blank. "I'm sorry! I didn't mean—"

To be condescending? "It's okay." She looked embarrassed, so he tried to mitigate the offense with a shrug. "I might not have known."

She gazed at him with a doubtful expression. Max nodded toward the University of Edinburgh campus. "I went there." He added, "I didn't finish. I had to drop out." *Did she need to know that?*

A fleeting look of surprise flashed on her face. "Oh. Well, college isn't for everyone."

"No, but it was for me—or would have been. But my dad had a stroke, so I quit school to run the pub."

"Oh, I'm so sorry!"

"It's okay. He's much better now, but the pub is too much to manage while going to school at the same time." Max couldn't believe he was opening up about this with a woman he'd only just met. Except they hadn't actually met. "I'm Max, by the way." He extended his hand.

She gave his hand a firm shake. "Olivia."

"Olivia."

"Well, Max, I don't want to keep you from your work."

"I'm the boss, so I take breaks now and then. I keep flexible hours—long, but flexible." *Why not just hand her your schedule?*

They shared a smile, then Max said, "So, where do you work?" *Now you're prying. It was bad enough when she thought you were clueless. Now she'll think you're a stalker.*

"Nowhere in particular. I've mostly finished my research, so now I'm just trying to piece it together. But to answer your question, I can work anywhere. I do some work at home—I mean the apartment I'm staying in while I'm here—but I enjoy a change of scenery now and then. Today, I thought I'd go to the Central Library."

"That's a great space."

"I love it! The reference library's my favorite, but I'm on a sort of rotation between that, the music library, and the Scottish library. And I like coffee shops. Know any good ones around here?"

"Have you tried the museum? There's one on the second level, the Balcony Café. And the National Gallery has a great café overlooking Princes Street Gardens. Apparently, we can't manage museums without coffee."

A smile lit her eyes. "I love sitting in your pub near the fire. It's a great place to go for a break from my quiet apartment."

"You know... the murmur of pub noise helps some people focus. I knew someone who used to sit by the fireplace—where you sat—to study." He cringed to hear himself admit he remembered not only Paulina but where she'd been sitting as well.

If Olivia thought it was weird, she didn't show it. "I can see why. You know, I would never do that in an American bar. But here, pubs have such a strong sense of community. And the atmosphere's so historic."

"Many of our pubs are older than your country."

Her eyes widened. "I hadn't thought of it like that. I guess that's what I love about The Red Rose."

"It's a great place to duck into from the weather." *The weather? Cut this short before she does.* "Well, enough about that. This is me heading back to the pub so you can get on with your day."

"Oh, right. Work."

"Busy day at the office?" He winced. His conversational skills seemed to have escaped him.

"Yeah, I just need to figure out where today's 'office' will be." She made air quotes then glanced at her hands with a wince.

Max caught himself gazing at her silky blond hair and looked away. "If you run out of options, I'm sure I could come up with a few more places you might like to work."

Olivia brightened. "I'd love your advice."

"Why don't you stop by later? I'll work up a list." He hoped his grin looked charming instead of desperate, which was how much he wanted to see her again.

Olivia nodded, but not as enthusiastically as he'd hoped. "Oh, okay. I could do that."

Their gazes lingered while Max tried to think of something witty to say. "Have a good day." *Have a good day? That'll charm her.*

"You too." She glanced over her shoulder and smiled.

He couldn't just leave it at that. She was walking away, and he didn't even have her number—not that she would have given it to him. Maybe he would work up the courage when she stopped by later. Except she hadn't promised to stop by after work. She'd just said that she could—just like he could bust out into a Highland sword dance right there on the sidewalk. But he wasn't about to do that. So he tamped down the hope of seeing her later.

"Cute ponytail."

Max flinched and turned to find Esme behind him. "Don't do that!"

"Do what?"

"Sneak up on me."

She grabbed his elbow and tugged him back toward the pub. "I didn't sneak. You were just... preoccupied."

He shot her a look of annoyance that should have shut down the topic, but she stared back, unfazed. He endured that for a handful of seconds before he looked away. "Busy street. Very distracting."

Her eyebrows wrinkled as a skeptical spark lit her eyes. "I said *preoccupied*, not *distracted*."

Not quite seeing where she was going with this, he shrugged. "Same thing."

"No... I don't agree. A distraction is fleeting, while a preoccupation lingers... like your eyes on that winsome American."

He wrinkled his face. "Winsome?"

"Aye, winsome—attractive, engaging, appealing..."

Esme hardly seemed to notice Max rolling his eyes and turning away. She continued as she followed him along the sidewalk, growing more singsongy with each word, "Lovely—no, loveable—adorable, sweet..."

Max grumbled. "Whatever."

Esme's mouth widened to a satisfied grin as he walked into the pub and left through the swinging doors to the kitchen. She called out, "Someone's in love!"

Warmed by the morning sun, Olivia smiled to herself as she walked to the library. Her dissertation was going well. She'd mapped out a rational plan for the day, completely confident she would achieve it. And Max had invited her to drop by after work. She drew a satisfied breath. *Well, why not?*

What was it about Scotland? The untamed landscape or the brooding sky? Everything seemed enchanted, as if it could all vanish into the mist only to reappear a century later. *Somebody's watched* Brigadoon *too many times.*

She stopped to wait for a light. *Maybe it's too magical here. Am I asking for trouble? What's wrong with stopping by a neighborhood pub—or getting to know Max?* She walked on but couldn't silence the nagging voice in her head.

Oh, nothing—except you just broke up with your boyfriend. And remember that doctorate? The one you won't get if you don't finish your work here? And don't forget that you're leaving at the end of the semester. You're in no state to begin a relationship.

Relationship? Who said anything about a relationship? I just find him attractive. It's a pub—a public house—after all. And he invited me. Not that it's like a date. It's a pub full of people. I'd just be one more patron.

Can you hear yourself?

She frowned. Her emotions were running amok. But it was normal to want a rebound relationship. Her subconscious just wanted a distraction.

Well, actually, I'm your subconscious, and that's not

what I want. What I want is to focus on work and not fall for some guy.

She told herself she wasn't falling, just passing the time. *Oh, look—the library. Let's see, shall we start in the reference or music library?*

It doesn't matter to me. The library won't break our heart.

Reference library. With a satisfied nod to herself, she headed upstairs.

7

By midday, Olivia needed some sunlight and air, so she headed to Greyfriars Kirkyard. She paused at the imposing iron gate that guarded the entrance. The place was said to be haunted, but she found it strangely inviting, with its park-like tranquility, lush foliage, and dappled shadows cast by leaves of ancient trees. Instead of reading as she'd planned, she was drawn along the pathways, studying the gravestones, each with unique if unusual designs worn down by centuries of harsh wind and rain. Skulls and crossbones intended to ward off evil spirits were common. Passing several spots perfect for sitting and reviewing her work, she followed the path to a corner of the yard. There, a charming herb garden thrived as a refreshing reminder of life. She'd come almost full circle when she took in the sight of an ominous mausoleum.

Footsteps stopped behind her. "Afraid of the ghosts?"

Olivia flinched and turned toward the familiar voice. "Max! No, just you! You startled me."

His eyes had that mirthful light she was growing to love. "I've been running. Hence the sweat."

She nodded. "It's nice weather for it—running, not sweating."

"Or both." He grinned.

She would never tired of his cobalt-blue eyes. She realized it was her turn to speak. "I got restless inside, so I came out to do some reading and editing."

"Always working."

That made her feel boring and bookish. She didn't know how to react. "Not always."

He appeared lost in thought over something she'd said. She was probably flattering herself. He could have been making a mental grocery list. Feeling unsure of what to say, she fell back on her usual tactic: escape. "Well, have a pleasant run." She glanced away toward the kirkyard.

"I just finished," Max said, "and I'm headed upstairs for a shower."

Shower? Olivia really wished he wouldn't feed her overactive imagination.

Apparently sensing her thought process, but thankfully not her thoughts, he explained, "I live upstairs over the pub."

"Oh. That's convenient."

He grinned. "Too convenient. It's a little like living at work. Sometimes, it's nice to get away."

"Oh, I know. Actually, that's why I'm here—in Scotland."

"From New York, right?"

"Yes." She was pleased he'd remembered. "I finished the coursework, but I can't seem to finish this dissertation. So the chance came up to apartment-sit, and I took it."

He nodded, looking genuinely interested. The guy was a good listener, but then, he was a bartender. That was what they did. He did it well—well enough that she continued. "I hoped getting away would help me focus."

"And has it?"

"It has, actually. I've fallen into a routine, and I've discovered a few places I'd like to sit and write." She nodded toward the kirkyard. "This one's new for me, but I've walked past it and wondered whether it might be worth a try. I'm always looking for fresh places to add to the rotation."

His expression brightened. "On sunny days like today, I used to go to the Meadows."

"I do love the Meadows, but I haven't tried studying there."

"On a day like today? It's brilliant." He pondered for a moment. "I'll show you. Let's have a picnic—I mean 'working lunch.'"

Wondering how much work she would get done, Olivia shook her head. But before she could speak, Max said, "Give me fifteen minutes to clean up, and I'll take you."

Olivia searched his eyes. "I can't ask you to do that."

"You didn't. I offered." When she looked hesitant, he said, "It's selfish. I'd like to hear more about your research—for professional reasons." When she furrowed her eyebrows, he explained. "Because I own a pub known for its live traditional music."

Olivia, what is your problem? He's asking you out!

"I might learn something."

She laughed. "I doubt that. I'm here to learn from you!"

"Even better." He gazed at her. "So you'll wait for me?"

His eyes revealed a vulnerable aspect she hadn't seen before. It disarmed her. "Okay. I'll find a place to sit and read while I wait."

"Just look out for the ghosts." he grinned.

"But... I thought that was only a sales tactic for the tours."

He lifted an eyebrow. "Could be. I wouldn't worry. You'll be fine."

But she didn't feel fine.

"I've got a better idea. Come with me. You can wait in the pub."

With a nod, she agreed, and they headed out of the kirkyard together and walked down the block to The Red Rose.

OLIVIA SAT at her favorite table, trying to read the same page again, but her thoughts were elsewhere. Conflicting emotions left her feeling awkward. Noah was out of her life, so she shouldn't feel guilty. Yet lingering thoughts haunted her. For so long, their shared routines had made her life feel stable and comforted her. With Max, she felt slightly off balance, never sure what to expect. Each moment filled her with wonder and anticipation of what he might say or do next. He didn't live large or make grand, sweeping gestures, but Olivia found his energy contagious.

The double doors to the kitchen swung open, and

Max walked in, having showered. His Fair Isle sweater highlighted his broad shoulders and tapered loosely to his blue jeans.

As he drew closer, she studied the intricately striped patterns. "Is that homemade?"

He nodded. "My mother. She stopped by this morning with some pies. Did I mention she does all our baking? Not that there's all that much. We're a pub, after all. But she tries to keep a couple of pies in the kitchen. Anyway, today, she brought me this sweater."

She wanted to run her fingers along the cables but had the good taste to resist. "It's gorgeous."

His eyes twinkled as he nodded. "She belongs to a knitting group. It was Fair Isle month."

"She sounds amazing."

Max chuckled. "Aye, she's a force to be reckoned with."

"And you adore her." Even as she smiled, an unexpected sadness bubbled up in her chest. She glanced away, but Max had seen it.

He studied her, worry etched on his face. "Are you okay?"

The sadness passed quickly, but she needed a moment to recover. "I'm fine. It's just... I lost my mother."

The tenderness in his eyes made her want to lean into that sweater, but his mother wouldn't appreciate her shedding tears all over her needlework. To shake off her vulnerable state, she took a deep breath and exhaled. "It was always just us. It's been over a year, but sometimes, it just hits me. Sorry."

His earnest reaction unsettled her, but when he

touched her shoulder, she was nearly undone. "Never apologize for loving your family."

His sympathetic gaze went too deep, so she avoided it. "She was all the family I had." When he was silent, she glanced up and nearly lost her composure. "Sorry."

Max leaned away with mock sternness. "What did I say?"

His kindness touched her in a way no one had since her loss. If she didn't blurt something out soon, she feared she might grab his sweater and kiss him. But they weren't ready for that, or at least he wasn't.

With bright eyes, she said, "So, what's for lunch?" *What's for lunch? That's the best you've got?*

He lifted a bag he'd apparently set on the table at some point, possibly just before he'd touched her shoulder. Her heart throbbed at the memory.

He extended his arm toward the door. "Shall we?"

The wide path that led walkers and bikers to the Meadows was flanked by historic university buildings on one side and glass-fronted apartments, including Olivia's, on the other. As they passed the second of two coffee shops, Max shared some antics he and his friends got into after weekly football matches at the Meadows.

He laughed and pointed to an area between two stone buildings. "Our first semester had barely begun when my mates and I decided we needed to make midnight football a thing."

"It sounds kind of nice, playing under the moonlight."

He raised an eyebrow. "In theory. The first time, we stopped by a couple of pubs on the way. By the time we got here, we discovered we'd lost the ball."

Olivia laughed. "I don't know much about sports, but I think the ball's pretty essential."

His mouth quirked at the corner. "And with that, you have proved yourself qualified to have refereed our game."

"The football game with no ball?"

"That didn't stop us."

"No?"

"Someone decided a discarded pizza box in the trash was a suitable substitute," Max said, shrugging with a hint of humor. "Needless to say, our judgment was clouded."

"I can imagine," Olivia replied, amused by Max's expressions.

Max continued, "We had just begun playing when it started to rain. At some point, the game shifted to waterskiing through puddles on the pizza box."

Olivia struggled to imagine. "How did that work out?"

"Even worse than you'd expect."

Olivia wished she could have been there. "Oh, I don't know. My expectations are pretty low."

"It all took a turn when I slipped and fell into the mud. My mates dubbed me Mud Max. Well, what else could I do but bring the others down with me? Before we knew it, we were all laughing, slipping, and falling—all coated in mud. It's one of my fondest memories from university."

Olivia's laughter faded as she wondered how hard it must have been to leave all that behind.

Max sighed. "Ah, the Meadows."

"And the end of midnight football." Olivia sighed.

Max leaned away with surprise. "Och, no! That

was just the beginning. Every full moon, or close to it, we were there with a football and a generous supply of rehydrating beverages—usually beer. Although there was one time one of our mates brought a leftover case of wine from a party his parents had recently thrown. But he didn't think to bring a corkscrew, so we had a contest to see who could best open a bottle of wine. There were extra points for creativity." He lifted an eyebrow. "I'll spare you the details of that for another day. It all ended when someone chose—with zero points for creativity— to use a rather large rock."

Olivia winced in anticipation.

Max nodded. "It shattered, of course. The cork flew in one direction while the wine flew everywhere else— mostly on us. The best part? A group of tourists took pictures of us, and we ended up on an American influencer's travel blog highlighting the best sights in Edinburgh." He chuckled, his eyes sparkling with amusement as he turned to her. "And here you thought I was a mild-mannered bartender."

Olivia couldn't stop smiling. "I never thought that! In fact, none of it is hard to imagine."

"Oh, aye? Well, I'd best not tell you about what we did in the spring."

He looked so amused that Olivia couldn't resist.

"You can't just drop something as intriguing as that without explaining!" One look at his roguish reaction made her wish she hadn't said it.

"Naked football."

Olivia slowly blinked, but closing her eyes only made it easier to imagine.

Max nodded, looking almost pleased with himself. "Full moon naked football."

She had no words. She was too busy trying not to swoon.

With a careless shrug, he said, "We're Scottish. We're halfway there in a plaid, so we didn't think much of it—until one time when a pub crawl stumbled upon us. We all scrambled to put on our clothes. Mind, we weren't shy, but we'd already landed on one travel blog. We didn't need to repeat it."

Olivia offered a distracted nod, but she couldn't get out of her mind the image of Max and his teammates in a naked football skirmish.

A burst of laughter tore Olivia from her musings. "We all scrambled to put our clothes back on, but our mate Bobby was so panicked, he put his pants on backwards and couldn't find the zip, so he just tripped along after us, clutching his trousers. From then on, he was Butt-Crack Bobby. Poor lad. We laughed about it for weeks—still do to this day whenever we get together."

Thinking of her own college years living at home, Olivia sighed. "The years I wasted in study carrels!"

"We did plenty of that, which was why we were so wild on the weekends. In all seriousness, Edinburgh was where I learned to appreciate the simple things in life, like a game of football and a good laugh with friends."

He stopped walking and turned to look into her eyes. "And to that, I can add picnic lunches."

If he didn't look away, she would succumb to a case of Victorian vapors.

With a grand arm gesture, he indicated a spot for their picnic. "How's this?"

"Lovely." She didn't even look. She was sold.

Max spread out a blanket on the sun-washed grass

and sat down to dig into the bag. There were sand-wiches and Scotch broth to fend off the autumn chill. After he asked, Olivia delved deeper into her reason for coming to Scotland, glossing over her breakup with Noah. As they sat chatting and eating their picnic lunch, an astonishing sense of well-being washed over Olivia. Everything in her life felt like a prelude to this perfect moment.

Max flexed his hands in surprise. "Oh! I almost forgot!" He reached into the bag and pulled out two covered containers. "Mum's pie!"

They finished the pie all too quickly. His mother could bake! After wrapping up their picnic, they parted ways—Max to the pub and Olivia to her flat. As he and Olivia paused on the sidewalk to say goodbye, Max's eyes twinkled with enthusiasm. "You can't go back to work without coffee."

Olivia smiled as she mentally tossed pages of her dissertation over her shoulder. "I wouldn't dream of it."

Max beamed. "Great. Come with me."

In a café, seated by a wall of windows, they lingered over their coffee for more than an hour. People walked by and went on with their day, but Olivia was too enraptured to notice.

Max left Olivia with a promise to show her one of his favorite places the next morning. Guilt gnawed at him as he headed back to the pub. He'd left Esme to manage alone—and she could—but it wasn't fair to burden her for the sake of his social life. As he stepped into the pub through the back door, he prepared himself for her reaction.

The minute he stepped inside the back door, she stuck her head in the doorway. "Oh, it's you." Her sarcastic tone was unmistakable. "Welcome back. I'd love to chat, but it's insane out there." Abruptly, she turned and went back to the bar.

Unable to leave it at that, Max followed, hoping to smooth things over. To his surprise, the pub wasn't busy at all. A few regulars sat at the bar, and a pair of tourists sat near the window. The rest of the pub was empty.

With a tinge of irritation, he said, "Poor you. You must be exhausted."

Her eyes sparkled. "Calm down. I was joking. It was fine. I barely noticed you were gone."

He frowned. "I'm not sure I like that."

Her eyes twinkled. "Well, you're hard to please today, aren't you?"

"Not really. In fact, I've had a very pleasant day so far." As soon as he spoke, he regretted it.

Esme folded her arms. "Oh really? That wouldn't have anything to do with your lunch companion, would it?"

"It has to do with spending an hour—"

"And a half."

He narrowed his eyes. "And a half in the sunshine."

She nodded expectantly. "With your new sweetheart."

He narrowed his eyes. "My new friend."

"Aye, right. Friend." Esme raised an eyebrow.

Max narrowed his eyes. "Aren't you due for a break?"

She didn't say any more, but the smirk she gave him on her way out was enough. Thank God she was gone. No one was more annoying than Esme when she knew she was right—not that Olivia was his sweetheart, but things seemed to be heading that way. And that was the problem. The more he grew to care for Olivia, the harder it would be to say goodbye. But no matter how hard he tried to deny his attraction to her, he was losing the battle. Each moment brought some additional aspect to light that drew him closer to her. Her sense of adventure in coming to Scotland alone was intriguing. Her work ethic was impressive. And then there was her smile. He had to stop now. It would only get worse.

A motion halfway down the bar caught his eye. "Connor!" Max hadn't even noticed when his friend walked in—probably because Connor wasn't wearing his usual always-unbuttoned white lab coat. Of average height, Connor had medium-brown hair and glasses. He had never been one to stand out, not because of his looks but because of his unassuming demeanor.

Once, Max made the mistake of mentioning to Esme that Connor lacked social awareness.

ESME SPRANG TO HIS DEFENSE. "He does not! He's a kind and considerate person."

Max reeled back. "Calm yourself. I'm just saying he doesn't always pick up on social cues."

Esme furrowed her eyebrows. "Such as...?"

Max meant women. When they approached Connor at the bar, he seldom picked up on their signals. Given Esme's reaction, explaining would only make matters worse. "Forget I said anything. He's a lovely man—charmingly nerdy."

Esme lifted her chin in defiance. "Nerdy? I think he looks like Clark Kent—if Clark Kent was a doctor. And Scottish."

That was when Max first suspected that Esme had feelings for Connor.

WITHOUT ASKING, Max grabbed a glass and had a pint ready for Connor soon after he sat at his regular barstool.

After a sip, Connor set down his beer. "So where've you been?"

Without thinking, Max said, "I just came back from a picnic. Oh! you meant..." He gestured toward where he'd been standing moments before, lost in thought.

"Aye, just now."

"Miles away." Well, more likely less than a mile.

A spark of amusement lit Connor's eyes. "And you're not quite back yet, are you?"

"If I'm honest, I am a wee bit lost. But I'll find my way back."

"It's been a while since I've seen that expression."

"What expression?"

"The look you get when you've found a new woman."

"Don't you start on me now!"

"Start what?" Connor looked sincerely confused.

Max gave him a weary look. "Esme's already gone down the list in some detail."

Connor furrowed his eyebrows. "What list?"

Esme joined them cheerily. "Did I hear my name?"

Max met her cheery expression with narrowed eyes then turned back to Connor. "Esme doesn't seem to think that a man and a woman could simply be friends."

"Well, they can..." Esme replied quickly, "but there's usually something else simmering under the surface."

Max turned away, but before leaving, he leaned close to Esme and murmured, "Like you and the doc?"

Esme's eyes popped wide open. Satisfied, Max headed down to a customer at the opposite end of the bar.

A few minutes later, Esme approached, came to a full stop, and glared. She drew in a breath.

Here it comes.

Esme's phone dinged, and Max exhaled his relief.

Esme looked at her phone, and her face underwent a complete transformation in a matter of seconds. "Oh, wow! Ainsley and Neil are engaged!" She looked at Max. "Excuse me." With a scowl, she added while dialing, "You're daft, by the way." She proceeded to FaceTime her friend Ainsley.

After emitting the highest-pitched squeals he'd ever heard come out of Esme, she said, "Wait. Max is here." She pointed the screen at Max.

Neil and Ainsley were pressed cheek to cheek, looking absurdly ecstatic.

"Congratulations, you two!"

Minutes later, the plans were cemented to celebrate at The Red Rose on the following Friday.

While Esme chattered away about Evites and a guest list, Max went to his office to plan for the event.

Two more college friends were moving on with their lives. He shook off the thought. *People fall in love and get married. It's part of life. Just not part of my life.* He looked around. This was his life and his legacy. At the center, his family and the pub formed a solid foundation. Here, he was rooted by history and as a Scotsman—a Scotsman alone. At the moment, the pub was cold comfort.

He headed out of the kitchen and made a quick stop at the bar. "Esme, I've got to go out. I won't be long."

She looked surprised but said nothing.

He had no errand to run; he just needed some air. Sometimes, the pub stifled him, and he had to go outside to breathe. After a brisk walk or a run, he would return ready to get on with his life. That didn't happen as much anymore. After all, he'd had years to reconcile himself to his lot in life. The strange thing about it was as a young lad, he used to watch his parents run the pub and think how much fun he would have when it was his turn. If they'd ever discussed his taking over, he couldn't remember. He'd just known it would be his one day. But somehow, he'd thought he could have both—university and a separate career. It wasn't until he started running the pub that he realized how impossible that would have been. If his life still had direction, he didn't control it.

He stopped at the George IV bridge and looked down at the Cowgate.

"Max? Hi."

"Hello." *Where did Olivia come from?* He'd been so wrapped up in his thoughts, he hadn't seen her approach.

He must have looked puzzled, because she said, "I was just on my way to the library when I saw you."

"Don't worry. I'm not going to jump." He didn't know why he said it. His dark mood must have gotten the better of him. Poor Olivia looked concerned, so he added, "I'm joking."

She wasn't laughing, but he couldn't blame her.

There was no way out except to change the subject. "Some uni friends just got engaged, so we're having a little celebration at The Red Rose on Friday. Why don't you come?" He was disappointed to see that she didn't look interested.

"That's so nice of you to include me..."

"But?" He attempted a casual smile, but it felt forced.

"I didn't say *but*."

"It's a no, then?" He could see on her face that she'd been thinking about it.

"I didn't say that either. I just think... I won't know anyone."

"I'll introduce you."

"Okay. I'm kind of buried in work, and I'm falling behind, but I'll try."

He nodded. "Okay." *So that's a definite no.*

She smiled a little too broadly. "Well, I'd better get going."

He nodded and looked at his watch. "Work?"

With a cloud of guilt, she nodded. "If I'm home, I might give in to temptation, so I'm going to the library."

"Oh, aye, the library."

She glanced down the street. "I love it, but I'm kind of stuck in a rut."

"That's no good."

She shrugged. "It's a character weakness. I should be able to work anywhere."

"If you like your surroundings, you'll be more productive."

"Exactly!"

For a moment, Max lost himself in her gaze. "I know a place. What time do you plan to get started tomorrow?"

"Eight."

Max winced and breathed in through clenched teeth. "Okay, eight. Stop by the pub, and I'll take you to my favorite reading place. It's outside, so it might be chilly first thing in the morning. Dress accordingly."

"Okay." Her furrowed eyebrows gave him the impression that she was duly intrigued.

"See you tomorrow."

Olivia's face brightened. "Tomorrow."

Their gazes locked for one perfect moment, then she walked away.

OLIVIA'S HEART was still pounding when she neared the library. The invitation troubled her, though. She knew he liked her, at least on some level, but The Red Rose was a historical neighborhood icon. Max and his family were well known in the community. They probably invited loads of people to this sort of event all the time. That didn't mean this invitation was anything special. Perhaps it was only her loneliness talking. Two weeks in Edinburgh with no one to talk to but Max and store clerks had made her unduly self-aware. That made going to the celebration the perfect opportunity to be social.

She stopped walking. *Get a grip.* The man behind her nearly ran into her. She quickly said, "Sorry!"

He sidestepped her, shot her an annoyed look, and went on his way.

She headed down the sidewalk, reminding herself she was not the shy college freshman she used to be. *It's okay. Keep working, go home, and live your life. Everything's going to be fine.* And it would. She knew that.

She arrived at the library and walked through the familiar doors to her comfort zone. Once settled, she donned her computer glasses and picked up where she'd left off earlier.

A page later, she had no idea what she had read. Her mind was on Max. She looked forward to going wherever he'd planned in the morning. However, the engagement party was another matter. She wasted another five minutes debating whether she'd feel out of place, then she got back to work.

No more thoughts of Max!

Until tomorrow.

F resh cups of coffee in hand, Max and Olivia turned the corner and headed down the Royal Mile. The only people walking along the usually busy street appeared to be locals on their way to work or tourists heading for an early tour bus pickup. Close to the end of the road stood Canongate Kirk, which Olivia had passed several times during her travels. Before they reached the church, Max paused on the sidewalk in front of an unassuming alley.

"This way." He lightly touched the small of her back and led her down the close. Through the wrought-iron gated entrance, they stepped into a small, secluded space.

"It's a secret garden!" she whispered with wonder.

"It is." He looked pleased by her reaction. With Max leading the way, they walked along a narrow path that led through the garden. On either side were small garden rooms, each with its own theme. She imagined the colorful flowers that must bloom throughout the summer, but a good deal of greenery lingered as if just for her.

At the end of the close, Max turned and swept his arm toward the space. "This is it—my reading escape from the city."

Warmth spread through her chest as she took in the peaceful surroundings. She could see why Max loved it. How many people must have walked past it, never knowing it was there? She'd done it herself.

Max said, "Find a bench, and I'll leave you to it."

She stood gazing at him while resisting the urge to embrace him. With restraint, she simply said, "Thank you."

Max's eyes shone. "I'm glad you like it." He gave her shoulder a light squeeze and left.

It took two days, but Olivia finally conceded that she had an all-out, not-going-away crush on Max Cameron. He might even like her too. There were signals, but they were open to interpretation. With a creative mind like Olivia's, those couldn't be trusted. She could write off the warm presence, the light in his eyes, and even the deep, lingering gazes, but she still felt his touch on the small of her back. Centuries prior, such things might have merely reflected chivalrous manners. Dunbar's Close certainly skewed her perceptions in an enchanting, otherworldly direction. But, along with the plants in that garden, her feet were rooted firmly in the present, as was her crush.

Viewed in a positive light, the best thing about crushes was that they weren't real. Better yet, they eventually faded. It might even be possible to enjoy this one while it lasted. Although, to be honest, her feelings for Max had completely surprised her, but she had since adjusted. After a few days to reflect, she was confident she had her heart under control. That accomplished, she could savor not only her feelings but the sight of Max—from afar. She could do that! The realization almost made her lightheaded. It wasn't as bad as she'd thought.

She didn't have to avoid Max. That would have meant having to avoid the pub, and she loved that place. From the first moment she'd stepped inside the old pub, the room's comforting aura and history lingered in the air. If she ignored the modern clothing of its current clientele, the dark wood, warm fire, and old smoke-stained beams might have convinced her she'd traveled through time. Add to that a live performance of centuries-old music, and she felt as though she'd come home.

She could think of no logical explanation for the powerful pull she felt to Scotland and The Red Rose. Psychologists theorized about genetic memory, citing how babies knew how to suckle without being taught. Olivia knew how to suck at writing her dissertation, despite being taught to do otherwise. Perhaps it was fate, but that explanation was too convenient. Whatever it was, it had driven her choice of research topic and brought her here.

By Friday, Olivia had put her crush on the back burner and accomplished more than she'd ever done in a week. She was typing away furiously when the librarian's voice interrupted her flow of thoughts. The library was closing in five minutes. Stunned, she looked at her watch and confirmed that it was five o'clock. That explained why she was hungry. She'd worked straight through from ten until five without eating.

As she walked over the George IV Bridge toward home, her stomach growled. A sudden craving for pub grub seized her. When she spied The Red Rose, she paused and shrugged. "Well, why not?"

The Friday-night crowd was gathered inside while musicians tuned up in the back. Four tables near the musicians had reserved signs on them, presumably for the engagement celebration. The gathering was smaller than Olivia had expected. Max hadn't really given her details. She knew it wasn't an official engagement party, but given how few reserved tables she saw, it appeared to be for a close circle of friends. Plus Olivia.

She exhaled. She was here now. If she changed her mind now and left, Max might see her, in which case, she would need an excuse. She didn't feel comfortable sitting down at the reserved tables before anyone else had arrived. Tucked away in a recessed nook, a small table sat empty. It was a great place to lie low and decide what to do. After draping her coat over her chair, she went to the bar to place her order of steak-and-ale pie with mashed potatoes and veg and a half-pint. She'd hoped Max would be there to make her feel welcome, but he wasn't there. Neither was Esme. Olivia got her half-pint and returned to her snug alcove. There, the pub took on a different aspect, bringing the Friday-night mood, with its laughter and music, into full relief against the dark ages-old woodwork. She leaned back, sipped her beer, and observed.

Within half an hour, the pub was teeming with people and lively conversation. More musicians straggled in and unpacked, leaving Olivia with nothing to do but let her gaze wander.

Then she saw him. Max seemed to appear as if stepping through a Scots mist, if the swinging kitchen doors constituted a mist. He leaned one elbow on the end of the bar with a pint in his hand. Before long, a flock of flirty females had gathered around him. That was when it struck her that she was just one of many drawn by his allure. It was no surprise, but she hadn't considered whether Max welcomed the attention. She'd been foolish to think she was special. He knew as well as she did that whatever they had wouldn't last. So what was she expecting?

She pulled her phone out and studied it intently. The musicians began playing, which was usually enough to send her into a zone, but her awareness was heightened and focused on Max. Tonight's musicians were especially good, but the cacophony of her own thoughts overwhelmed the sound. There went her plan to enjoy her crush from afar. Max looked busy, probably with his school friends, so she sank back behind a pillar that partially concealed her and sipped her half-pint while she planned her escape. She couldn't just leave without saying hello. So she would sip her pint and keep an eye out until he left his friends and went to the bar. She could say hello and fade away toward the exit.

Mentally rehearsing each step spoke to the pathetic nature of her state of mind, but she dismissed the thought. Exhaling, she rubbed her forehead. She was wasting so much energy on a man she barely knew. Had she learned nothing from Noah? But Max was nothing like Noah.

In his defense, Noah had helped her escape from

her grief. He had also distracted her from her studies, which hadn't worked out so well. Since she'd come to Scotland, she hadn't needed or wanted to escape from her thoughts. She was content here. Max only added to that—or so she'd thought until now. *What if my well-being is based on a self-created fantasy?*

With a sigh, she realized Max was taking up too much real estate in her head, real estate that she needed for work. If things were different, if she weren't under pressure to finish her PhD, and if she weren't going home, she might let her thoughts and her heart dwell on Max. But things were not different. She needed to focus.

Esme appeared by her table. "So how was Dunbar's Close?"

Olivia smiled. "Great. I got a lot of work done."

"Max told me he took you there and just left you. That wasn't very gentlemanly of him."

Olivia shook her head. "That was the plan all along. I like reading outside, and he thought I'd enjoy Dunbar's Close."

"You and Max. Two workaholics. You're perfect for each other." She raised her eyebrows knowingly. "And you're his type."

"His type?" Olivia asked, intrigued.

Esme shrugged. "Pretty and blond. So, what is it you came here to study?"

Olivia was still stuck on the concept of Max's type, but she caught up quickly. "Traditional Scottish folk music."

"Well, you're in the right place, but why Scottish folk music in particular?"

"I've always loved the songs. I majored in voice, and

my mother was Scottish." Olivia finished the thought with a shrug.

"What songs do you know?" Esme asked.

Olivia considered the question. "Well, there's 'Loch Lomond.' I have a fond memory of my grandfather singing it to me when I was a young child. Let's see... 'Auld Lang Syne,' of course. And probably my favorite —'Ae Fond Kiss.' I actually sang that as an encore at my graduate recital."

Esme's face lit up. "You should sing for us sometime."

Olivia shook her head, but Esme persisted. "You should! That's how it works here. Anyone can join in and perform."

"I don't really sing anymore." Not only that, but she hadn't even thought about singing in public for months.

"Why not?" Esme asked.

"I don't know. I got busy teaching and working on my dissertation, so it just kind of fell down the priority list."

Esme glanced over at Max and leaned toward Olivia conspiratorially. "That's his get-back-to-work look. I'd better go." She shrugged and left.

Olivia quickly dismissed the thought of singing but appreciated Esme's effort to include her. What she couldn't dismiss was Esme's remark about Olivia being Max's type. She closed her eyes for a moment and reminded herself to stop longing for the impossible. But as soon as she opened her eyes, her attention went straight to the bar. There he was, pouring drinks and chatting with customers, most of them female. Not that he was doing anything wrong. His charm was good for business. But Olivia's business, her career,

would suffer if she didn't clear her head—and heart—
soon.

HAVING HIRED extra help for the evening, Max was
free to hang out at the end of the bar and enjoy celebrating with Ainsley and Neil. Olivia never showed up,
but he hadn't expected her to. Still, that hadn't kept him
from watching for her every time the door opened.

The festivities were in full swing when Paulina
walked in. Max leaned over to Esme. "What's she doing
here?" University years with Paulina flashed before him
then paused on the scene in which she broke his heart.

Esme winced. "Ainsley asked, and I couldn't say no.
After all, Paulina is her maid of honor."

"You could've warned me."

Esme looked pained, but not as pained as he felt.
She said, "I honestly didn't think she'd actually come up
from London—especially knowing we'd be here. How
was I to know she'd head straight for Kings Cross
Station and catch a train?"

He glared.

Unable to endure Max's silence, Esme said, "Just
avoid her."

He narrowed his eyes.

"I'm sorry. I didn't know what to do. If I told you,
and she didn't show up, it would've ruined your
evening."

"Unlike now."

Esme's eyebrows were stuck in a furrowed position.
"Yeah, I know. A rail strike would've been nice." She
sighed. "Maybe you could just... ignore her."

Max stared blankly at her then went into the kitchen. Esme was right. He just had to ignore her.

The double doors from the bar swung open. "Hello, Max."

Without looking, he knew who it was. "Paulina." He braced himself and turned around to face her. *Take the high road. Be civil then move on. Separately.*

She said softly, "It's been a long time." Her steady gaze was no accident. She had to know how it knotted his stomach.

Max managed a nod but couldn't trust himself to speak.

She averted her eyes then looked back at him. "Well, it's good to see you. I mean it."

To his surprise, he didn't sound angry or hurt as he said, "Ainsley and Neil are in there. I'm sure they'll want to see you. Excuse me." Without waiting for her reaction, he turned and went upstairs to his flat.

Barricading the door came to mind, but he knew she wouldn't follow him. That wasn't her style. Max paced the full length of the room, knowing he couldn't hide forever. This was his party. He was the host. But he needed a minute. Esme could hold down the fort.

After all these years, he wasn't sure how he felt. It wasn't the heartsick, roiling ache of the past. At least that much was over, but new feelings surprised him. The initial knee-jerk nausea and resentment had subsided, and he resigned himself to her presence. After all, as a member of the wedding party, she had a right to attend. He stopped pacing.

Why should I care? He took a breath and exhaled. The emotion—or lack of it—was liberating. *I don't care*

*what she does. I'd rather not see her, but she's there. So
are my friends, and I'm going to enjoy them.*

Minutes later, he walked into the bar. The music,
especially lively, had prompted many to dance—even
Esme. A hand grasped his. *Paulina.*

"Come on. For old times' sake!" She flashed the
winning smile she'd perfected.

"No, thank you. I'm not in the mood." His protests
were lost in the music's swell and chattering voices.
Ainsley stopped dancing with Neil long enough to
grasp Max's and Paulina's hands and finish the job.
Reluctant to make a scene, Max endured a lively cèilidh
dance until it transitioned seamlessly into a ballad.
Having done his time, Max caught Paulina's wrists as
she circled his neck and swayed to the music. Before he
could remove her arms and make his escape, she
stepped closer and kissed him.

Max recoiled. "What are you doing?"

"Max, remember how we used to be?"

The longing in her eyes highlighted his own lack of
affection. Those feelings were gone. "Paulina, what we
had is over. It will always be over."

As he retreated to the bar, he caught Esme's eye.
She nodded toward the exit, where blond hair caught
the light. He recognized the raincoat.

Esme said, "Olivia."

Still reeling from his encounter with Paulina, Max
couldn't quite piece together what it meant. "Is she
okay?"

Esme grimaced. "She seemed fine until she saw you
making out with your ex-girlfriend."

"We weren't—wait. That upset her?"

Esme rolled her eyes.

THE NEXT MORNING, Olivia finished a video conference with her advisor. It went well. Her work was back on track. Dr. Lamanski was pleased. The strategy behind her semester in Scotland was working.

Her situation with Max, sadly, was not. Her rebound guy had too much baggage. Last night had made that painfully obvious. But that wasn't the point. Fretting over Max served no purpose. Baggage or not, he could never be hers. Come December, the only thing close to her heart would be her PhD.

10

Droplets of rain trickled down the glass of the front windowpanes. It had been seven days since Max last saw Olivia, but he kept hoping he would see her.

Esme shook her head with pity. "You've got to stop watching that door. If she comes in, she'll come in—whether you watch it or not."

She was right, which was not always an endearing quality.

"Why don't you text her? Just say you haven't seen her and hope she's okay."

"Brilliant idea, but I don't have her number." She was trying to help, but she didn't.

Esme peered closely at him. "You're joking."

"If I were, at least one of us would be laughing."

Esme shook her head slowly. "In that case... I guess you could hang out on her corner until she shows up. I think I saw a movie about that."

"Involving a stalker?"

"No! It was romantic."

"Well, this is not. And I don't know her address."

Esme dropped her cleaning rag onto the bar. "Wow, Max. You have really lost your touch with the ladies."

He had no retort, just a scowl.

Esme sighed. "Okay, fine. Just keep staring outside, 'cause that's working. While you're doing that, I'll do something constructive, like add a log to the fire to get rid of this chill in the air."

After stoking the fire, Esme went back behind the bar. "You'll think I've gone daft, but have you thought about telling her how you feel?"

The door opened, and Max flinched then relaxed. It was only Connor. As his friend approached the bar, Max murmured to Esme, "Not a word about this."

She frowned. "You have so little faith in me."

He muttered, "It has nothing to do with faith. I just know you."

"Apparently not." She flashed a bright smile at Connor. "Hello! What'll it be, the usual?"

Before Esme could reach for a glass, Max said, "I'll get it."

"Thank you." Connor set down his umbrella and sat at the bar. "When I finished my shift at the hospital, the sun was shining through the windows! But by the time I got to the door, this happened." He waved his hand toward the rain outside and smiled helplessly.

Esme flashed a bright smile. "Who needs sunshine when you've got us?"

Max set down a pint in front of Connor then nodded toward Esme. "Someone's had too much coffee."

She shot a sarcastic smile at Max. "Maybe someone just has a more positive outlook."

Connor fished some money out of his pocket and handed it to Max, but Esme reached out and took it. All traces of sarcasm gone, she said, "Max, I got this. She's outside. Run and catch her."

Max froze as Olivia walked past the window, gripping her umbrella with both hands like a shield against the wind and driving rain. *Should I?* If she didn't want to see him, then running after her like a maniac would just make things worse. On the other hand, if she wasn't avoiding him, then this might be his best chance to explain. Of course, that wouldn't be easy. He'd only seen her leave after Paulina's kiss. He'd assumed all the rest. What if he'd misread everything?

As she disappeared from view, a sharp shove in his back settled it. Esme pushed him again. "Go after her, man!"

Max sprang into action. Halfway down the block, he caught up with her. "Olivia!"

She stiffened then stopped. She turned with a smile that was warm but forced.

Rain drizzled down Max's wet hair and face.

Olivia lifted her umbrella so that it covered them both. "Here." She waited for him to say something.

You're the one who came bounding after her like a dog with a Frisbee. Say something! He brushed dripping hair from his face. "We've missed you." *Did that sound desperate?*

She looked down. "Well, I... uh, couldn't..."

"Esme said you stopped by."

She looked puzzled.

"At the party."

She winced but quickly recovered. "Oh." She nodded.

"If I'd seen you... Well, I did see you, but not till you walked out the door."

"That's okay. You looked... busy, and I guess I wasn't in the mood for a crowd."

He steeled himself. If he didn't say it now, he might not have another chance. "Whatever you saw—"

"It's none of my business."

"Paulina—"

She lifted her palm to stop him. "That's okay." She glanced down the street. "I should really be going." She turned and took a step then another.

"Wait!" Max stepped toward her. "Can we talk?"

It was a simple question, but Olivia couldn't decide what to say.

Max tilted his head toward the pub. "Let's get out of the rain and go sit by the fire."

THE WARMTH of a fire was appealing enough, but his vulnerable look finished the job. Against her better judgment, she said, "Okay."

Esme raised her eyebrows as Max and Olivia walked in through the door. Max touched Olivia's elbow to guide her past the bar to her favorite table by the wood burner, but Connor said hello to Olivia, so she stopped.

Max introduced them then watched them exchange small talk, wishing he'd brought her in through the back door. But that would have been weird, so he stood beside her at the bar and waited.

Connor extended his hand. "Nice to meet you. So,

Esme tells me you're here for a semester. What are you studying?"

Max couldn't believe Connor. Had he not seen Max rush outside, into the pouring rain, after Olivia? Did he really think this was time for a chat?

Equally oblivious to Max's plight, Olivia said, "I'm working on my doctoral dissertation on traditional Scottish folk music."

Connor leaned forward with interest. "The Red Rose is one of the best pubs in the city for music."

Thank you, now stop talking. Max groaned inwardly.

Olivia nodded. "So I hear."

Connor and Olivia exchanged an appreciative nod about the music, while Max stood by helplessly. This was not how this was supposed to go. At all.

Max's voice came out a little too loud. "Aye, well, I'm sure you and Esme have lots to talk about. We'll let you two get on with it." Ignoring Esme's sharp, questioning look, he touched Olivia's elbow and gestured toward her favorite table.

Before he could lead her away, Esme, now visibly ruffled, chimed in. "You two have a lot in common with your doctoral studies. Connor's a doctor."

Olivia said, "Oh, what kind?"

Now completely frustrated, Max blurted out flippantly, "He's a sex doctor."

Olivia's eyes widened, then her eyebrows drew together.

Max tried to tamp down his impatience, but the situation was irritating him. Still, Connor didn't deserve this. The poor guy was just being pleasant, but Max needed to talk to Olivia.

Connor said, "Actually, I'm an ob-gyn."

Olivia nodded, now understanding.

Max said, "Yeah, he makes babies."

Connor's eyebrows drew slightly together. "I don't make them. I just deliver them. They arrive preassembled."

Olivia shot a questioning look at Esme, while Connor peered at Max with a similarly questioning, if more emphatic, expression.

Ignoring him, Max said. "He's a people postie."

"A postie?" Olivia asked.

Max explained, "Postal operative... mail deliverer."

After a polite laugh, she said, "Oh, right."

Max couldn't stop himself. "He's basically a stork with an advanced degree." *You're being a jerk.*

Connor shook his head as if to say ignore him. "Max can't seem to get past the idea that my workplace is called the NHS Lothian's Sexual and Reproductive Health Service."

Esme added, "Max can't get past the word 'sexual' without his mind wandering."

When the three of them laughed, Max protested. "Guys, Olivia doesn't know me that well. You'll scare her away." They all thought he was joking. He wasn't.

Max blamed it on nerves, but he couldn't explain that to Olivia, since she was the source of his inner torment. He was inwardly berating himself when something miraculous happened.

Esme said, "Max is right."

That caught Max's attention.

She continued, "We're not scary once you get to know us." Her eyes twinkled as she cast a quick glance at Max. "You should stay after closing and have breakfast with us." She looked at Max with a look that could only mean, *You're an idiot, but I'm a merciful saint. Thank me later.*

He was slow to pick up the cue. "Right. You should."

Sudden dismay filled Esme's eyes. "Oh, but I won't be able to make it." Seeing Max's questioning look, she added, "I've got something."

Max eyed her skeptically. "At one in the morning?"

Esme straightened her posture and said proudly, "I have a surprisingly busy social calendar." Then she walked away.

Seeing Olivia's confused look, Max said, "I'm sorry. Subtlety is not Esme's strong suit."

Olivia said, "I understand. She's a good friend."

"Aye, but—"

She interrupted, "And you are a very nice guy. So I'll let you off the hook for breakfast."

She reached for her backpack, but he touched her hand. "Don't go." He exhaled. "Now we've both scared you away."

She slid her hand from his, but at least she'd let go of her bag. She looked quizzically at Max. "Why is Esme so eager to fix you up?"

With a tolerant smile, he shrugged. "She feels sorry for me."

Olivia leaned back and stared with disbelief. "Why? You've got women lined up at the bar, practically elbowing each other to get your attention."

He looked down to hide his embarrassment. "College students. Not exactly my type."

She tilted her head curiously but said nothing.

Max couldn't take the silence, so he explained. "I'm not good relationship material."

Her eyes sparkled. "You seem nice enough to me."

Their eyes locked. Something passed between them. He couldn't have explained it, but it felt electric. Then she looked away, and the moment was over.

Connor left them and headed toward the men's room.

"Did you want to talk to me about something?" Olivia asked, catching him off guard. "Outside, you said..."

"Right. Yes. Yes, I did. Yes..." *Stop saying yes.* "Let's go sit by the fire."

Esme called out, "I'll bring you both some Scottish coffee."

Max smiled to himself. Esme had her moments. When Max and Olivia were settled by the fire, coffee drinks in hand, Max broached the subject hesitantly. "The other night... what you saw..."

Olivia would not meet his gaze. This was not going well.

Just say it. "I didn't kiss her. She kissed me."

Her eyes flitted toward his. "You don't need to explain."

"But I want to." That came out louder than he'd intended. "Sorry. This is coming out all wrong."

Olivia said, "It's okay."

Did she mean it's okay that I practically shouted at her or that I kissed Paulina?

She looked at him, which he counted as progress. "You told me you're not good relationship material."

He wanted to kick himself for that one. "Different context. When I said that, I was talking about... never mind. My point is—the other night, Paulina got carried away, but it's over between us. It's been years. I don't want to go back there."

Olivia said gently, "It's okay. You don't owe me anything. We're friends."

Friends? That felt like a massive demotion. Until now, he'd thought they shared feelings. But apparently not. The other night when she left, he assumed seeing him with Paulina had upset her. But maybe she'd just left because she wanted to go. Was it really that simple? Had he misread the situation?

He proceeded carefully. "As friends... I want you to know that my plans for the evening did not involve my ex-girlfriend. She had a few drinks that went to her head, and she got nostalgic."

Olivia nodded, apparently unaffected by his explanation. "Well, good. I'm glad we ran into each other."

He couldn't help it. He smiled. *Well, actually, I ran after you, but...*

She surprised him by returning his smile. "I enjoy being with you."

He suppressed the urge to sigh with relief. "I feel the same about you. The other night, I wanted to spend time with you."

She sighed and attempted a smile. "I would love getting to know you. You're fun, interesting..."

He liked where this was going.

"But distracting."

He shook his head, not understanding, but Olivia forged on. "Before I came here—to Scotland—I went through some things, mainly losing my mother. Then my schoolwork suffered. I guess breaking up with my boyfriend was part of it too." She looked into his eyes.

"Anyway, it's so magical here. Edinburgh is so different that... I just got a little detached from reality." She looked up as though searching for words. "I need to stay focused on my project."

"I would never get in the way—"

"You haven't! It's all me. I let myself get side-tracked." Her eyes softened. "If you weren't so charming..."

He clenched his fist. "Curse you, charm!" He was only half joking. What she saw as charm was, in fact, his fascination with her.

Warmth poured from Olivia's eyes until he couldn't look anymore. He lowered his eyes to her soft hands and imagined lifting those hands to his lips.

She said gently, "I still want to be friends. I just need some space."

His stomach churned. *Space?* Was she really breaking up with him before they'd even gotten together? He lifted his chin but couldn't manage a nod. Silent agony stretched between them until he couldn't take the stillness. "There's no pressure. I'm here. I'm not going anywhere."

She threw in a sharp breath. "But I am. That's the problem."

Why was she saying this now? There was something between them. Why not give it a chance?

Olivia reached over and squeezed his hand. "I'll see you around."

She was gone, and he couldn't stop her because the wind had been knocked out of him.

11

E sme and Connor watched Olivia leave, then they exchanged a look. Esme whispered, "That didn't go well, from the looks of it."

Connor shook his head. "Relationships."

"They're not always easy."

Connor raised his eyebrows. "I wouldn't know. I've never really had one."

Esme suppressed her shock.

He looked at her as though he'd heard her thoughts. "It's not like I set out to be a dating loser."

"You're not!"

"Please. I am fully aware of what I am."

"And what's that?"

"A nerd. No, don't try to argue the point."

"But you're not a nerd or a loser! You're amazing—" She stopped just short of revealing her feelings then lowered her voice. "You're an amazing guy."

"Yeah, that's what my dates all say before they tell me it's not working out."

Her eyes softened. "Dating's hard—so I've heard. I haven't been on one lately."

"You could try the dating app I use."

Esme grimaced. "I'm not a dating app type."

Connor shrugged. "If it weren't for dating apps, I wouldn't have any dates."

"Yeah, but... never mind."

"I know. It hasn't worked yet, but it's only a matter of time."

Esme wanted to agree, but she couldn't.

Connor said, "I'm sure you'd have better luck. You're not socially awkward like I am."

"What are you talking about? I love talking to you. You're an interesting guy!"

"I'm an interesting guy to talk with sitting in a bar, but dating-wise, I just haven't had enough practice. While everyone else was perfecting their game, I was in a library study carrel with my nose in medical books. Now look at me."

Esme did look at him like she had so many times, from his neatly trimmed light-brown hair to the tortoise-shell glasses that brought out the green in his eyes. They were soft and impossibly deep, like the sea. She could drown in those eyes. She realized she was staring and meant to avert her eyes, but her gaze drifted down to his mouth.

Her lips parted. Barely able to breathe, she said, "You don't need any practice. You're you. That's enough—more than enough!" She drew in a breath, afraid she'd said too much.

Connor chuckled. "Tell that to my dates."

Esme smiled gently. "It can't be that bad."

"Oh, it can."

"I'm sure there are plenty of women who'd love to date you."

"Great, give me their phone numbers."

She recited her own in her mind then looked into his eyes. "You'll find your perfect someone. In the meantime, you've got me to talk to." She smiled cheerfully to hide her true feelings.

With a gentle smile, Connor thanked her. "If I'm honest, it's not always my fault."

"Of course not!"

Connor hesitated. "I never talk about it. I'm not sure why I'm telling you, except maybe it's like therapy. It helps to talk it out."

"I'm a bartender, which makes me practically a registered professional therapist—absent the legal registration."

Connor humored her with a nod. "My last date, Saturday—I've been trying to forget it. Another dating app meeting, but we had something. She was smart, funny, and pretty."

"Of course." Esme tried not to smirk.

"We chatted for almost an hour." He shook his head helplessly. "And we made plans to meet for drinks."

"That sounds great!" Esme tried to be positive for his sake.

"It was great. At first." Connor took a sip of his beer. "We sat at the bar and started talking. I thought I'd finally met someone I could go on a life journey with —at least a short one—to a second date. Which would be a first." He sighed. "It was going so well. Then... she sneezed."

Esme raised an eyebrow. "That's it? She sneezed? That's your disaster?"

Connor grimaced. "It wasn't just a sneeze. It was... massive. Like a Doberman's bark... sort of mixed with a donkey's bray."

Esme considered it. "So she's a loud sneezer. But otherwise, you said she was great. I mean, everyone's got their wee flaws."

"But her flaws involve mucus, like a spray bottle set on jet stream—a jet stream of snot."

"Ew!" Esme lifted her palms to stop him. "That's enough! I get it!"

Connor looked down and shook his head slowly. "Don't get me wrong. In my line of work, I see more than my share of body fluids. But outside of work—I mean, everyone needs some downtime."

Esme tried to look sympathetic.

"I'd barely recovered from the epic sneeze when she wiped her nose with her fingers then reached for the chips and salsa we were sharing."

Esme cringed. "Oh!" She shuddered. "Oh, no!"

"Oh, yes. And then—"

Esme cringed. "No, not more."

Connor continued. "She took out her phone and, with her air-drying snot-fingers, started swiping through photos..."

Esme had to stop him. "That's okay. Just say selfies. I don't need to know which body parts."

"Cat."

"What?" Esme leaned back, confused.

"Her cat."

Esme hadn't expected that. "Oh... Well, cats are cute."

"To a point. But this was... intense. There were costumes and sets. Glamor poses."

Esme's mouth opened, but she couldn't make words come out.

Connor looked blankly at Esme. "They weren't just random outfits. Marie Catoinette was dressed in the period costume of each of her past lives."

Esme couldn't hold in a laugh, but she quickly suppressed it.

Connor looked over his glasses. "Guess how many?"

"Nine?" Esme's laugh exploded.

Connor joined in. Esme tried to stop laughing and look sympathetic, but the more she tried not to, the worse it grew.

Between laughs, Connor said, "She listed each one."

"Dare I ask?"

"Why not? If I can't use my freakish gift for auditory recall, what good is it? I mean, other than medicine. Let's see. There's Furrence Nightingale, Marie Purrie, Cleopawtra..."

"I would love to see those costumes."

"No, really. You wouldn't. Let's see... Sojourner Mewth, Elizabeth Catty Stanton, Daphne DuPurrier..."

"Of course."

"Yeah. And the last two... Oh, yes. How could I forget? Jane Meowsten and Emily Kittenson."

When Esme's laughter had subsided, she sighed. "Oh, Connor. I'm so sorry."

Connor shrugged and said wryly, "But it's not like she made it all up. Her cats went through recovered-memory therapy. So their past lives are basically facts, and facts don't lie."

"Cats don't either." Esme's eyebrows drew together

as she shook her head slowly. "So... I guess date number two...?"

"Not gonnae happen."

WHEN CONNOR HAD GONE, Esme found a few quiet moments to approach Max. "What happened?"

He cast a sideways glance toward her. "I don't want to talk about it."

"It might help."

His expression darkened. "My crying on your shoulder won't do anything except satisfy your curiosity."

"Well, that's just not fair!"

He snapped back, "Life's not fair."

Esme narrowed her eyes. She had known Max long enough to know when to leave him alone. But she couldn't help herself. "Max, I'm sorry, but you two are so good together."

He glared at her enough to make her feel uncomfortable. "No, we are not good together, because we aren't together, and we never will be."

"But you could be. No, you should be. She's so nice but so lonely and lost, and God knows you're lonely."

"But not lost," Max added sarcastically.

"Fine. If you won't listen to reason..."

"Esme, I didn't have a choice."

"Aye, right. As if anyone's ever dumped you—well, except for Paulina. Too many disappointed lassies have sat at this bar and cried over you."

"Och, your bum's out the window."

She shook her head slowly.

Max rolled his eyes in defeat. "I don't know what you're talking about. All I can tell you is that Olivia broke up with me. Which was the fastest breakup on record since we weren't really together."

"Maybe not, but there was something. Everyone could see it."

"Everyone?"

"Aye, everyone... the regulars. You're their favorite soap opera."

"You lot all need hobbies."

Esme couldn't disagree. "Aye, we do. But we want you to be happy."

Max was at a rare loss for words. Of the series of expressions that crossed his face, the clearest was disbelief.

"Come on, Max. They might be your bar patrons, but they're also your friends."

She was pleased to see he'd calmed down enough to listen. "You know, Olivia could use some friends, and we're the only ones she has here."

He gazed upward as though searching for words. "Let me explain this again. She broke up with me. It's not what I wanted, but I have to respect her decision."

Esme wasn't ready to give up, but she didn't know what else to do.

Max scowled. "Stop staring at me like I'm a lost puppy."

She didn't appreciate that, but she chose not to respond.

Esme wasn't sure what she had done, but Max's mood shifted. He snapped at her. "Look, just because things are looking up for you and Dr. Ladyparts doesn't mean you can take me on as a project."

"Oh! First of all, ew! Second, his name's Connor Begbie—Dr. Begbie to you! And things are not looking up! Why would I want them to? Connor's a customer."

"Oh, come on, Esme. You've had a crush on him for as long as I can remember."

She opened her mouth to protest, but words wouldn't come out. Despite giving her best effort to stare him down, Max's eyes bored through her until she gave up.

Esme fumed. "If you tell anyone..."

His eyes softened. "I haven't yet, have I?"

She hoped he didn't know how the kind look in his eyes always defused her anger. It was partly why they'd stayed friends so long. They might argue like brother and sister, but they always came back to this place. They were here for each other.

"He doesn't like me. I mean, not in that way. I'm like his bartending sister. It's my gift and my curse. Beloved by all but desired by none."

Max's eyes filled with warmth. "Well, he's an idiot, then."

With a helpless shrug, she said, "It couldn't possibly be my fault."

"Or mine with Olivia."

Esme's eyes twinkled. "I mean, look at us. We're perfect!"

"Yeah, we are." He hooked an arm around Esme's shoulders and gave her a kiss on the forehead.

12

Olivia was typing away at a passage on vocal technique in Scottish traditional music when her phone dinged with a text. *Dr. McNabb?* She hadn't spoken with her since moving into the apartment. A sudden panic gripped her. She hoped Dr. McNabb wasn't coming home early. Olivia loved her apartment too much. Her fears were soon put to rest as she read.

Olivia, hello! I hope you're enjoying the apartment. I just wanted to let you know there's a trad band you should hear, if you can. The Loch Ness Minstrels will be at the Silver Stag in Old Town tonight. I know them and love them. Of course, one of them, Archie, is my son, so I'm biased. But others consider them quite good as well. If they're booked and you can't get in, drop my name—and be sure to tell them I said hello!

Olivia immediately answered: *I will! Thanks for the heads-up!*

Having had two highly productive days, Olivia was feeling so accomplished that she decided to treat herself to dinner out. She looked up The Silver Stag on her phone. They served dinner, so she made a reservation. She hadn't been to any music pubs other than The Red Rose, so this would nudge her out of her comfort zone.

As she thought about The Red Rose and Max, a small heart pang came and went. With a sigh, she let her thoughts linger on him for a moment. For two days, she'd focused on work. Not that Max didn't come to mind often. But she made a point of redirecting her thoughts to her studies, and her strategy worked—at least part of the time.

So why do I miss him so much?

She stopped, took a deep breath, and packed up her computer. Tonight, she would dine well and be inspired by the outstanding music. Best of all, it would help get her mind off Max.

Tucked around the corner on a side street off the Royal Mile stood The Silver Stag. If the pub's name weren't enough, one step inside confirmed it had a hunting lodge theme. The eyes of the wall-mounted animal faces followed her, but warm and inviting humans greeted her. After quickly finding her reservation, a young man in a kilt led her to a cozy table across from a dumbwaiter that went to the kitchen below. Soft lighting cast a welcoming glow over the space, bringing out the texture of the carved wall panels.

The pub lived up to its name. Antlers, animal skins, and an array of weapons from over the ages adorned the walls. In short, it had to be a vegetarian's nightmare. But from a historical and cultural aspect, Olivia found it fascinating. At the moment, though, the menu in her hands was her primary interest. It promised hearty game and fish dishes along with an impressive variety of ales and wines. Scottish salmon sounded perfect, so she ordered it and leaned back to relax. *Thanks again, Dr. McNabb!*

By the time Olivia finished her dinner, she felt like the evening had already been perfect. Half an hour before the music began, she settled her bill and moved to a room in the back, where the band would perform. The musicians had arrived and were setting up when Olivia approached an older woman wearing a colorful patchwork skirt and a bright-red blouse. Olivia waited while the woman bent down to a weathered leather case and pulled out a vintage accordion with mother-of-pearl buttons.

Olivia said, "Excuse me."

The woman rose. "Yes?"

"I'm a friend of Dr. McNabb's."

Her face lit up. "Are you now? Well, it's lovely to meet you. I'm Isla Campbell."

They shook hands and chatted a bit about Dr. McNabb, then Olivia said, "I see that you're busy. I won't keep you."

Isla set her accordion on a chair, looked about, then leaned toward Olivia. "If I'm honest, we do need to set up, but sit over there at the musicians' table. We'll chat after this set, and I'll introduce you to the others."

Olivia thanked her and, given how crowded the pub was, gladly took her up on her offer to sit at the musicians' reserved table. After securing a half-pint from the bar, Olivia sat down and took it all in. The music was minutes away, and the place was packed. Sporting an old hand-carved fiddle was a lanky man with wild, curly hair and a bushy beard, wearing old jeans and a plaid flannel shirt. A petite woman with a loose auburn pony-tail cascading down her emerald-green dress set two tin whistles on the floor. She arranged them by size then picked up a set of smallpipes. Beside her stood a burly, barrel-chested man with a thick red beard, a bodhrán drum in one hand and a pint of ale in the other. The fifth, and the only one young enough to be Dr. McNabb's son, was a handsome young man with dark-brown hair and dark, piercing eyes. He breezed in, helmet in hand and an acoustic guitar case slung cross-wise over his black-leather-jacket-clad back. He greeted the others. The drummer pointed toward the musicians' reserved table, and he headed that way. Spotting Olivia, he flashed a smile so charming, Olivia wondered if he'd mistaken her for somebody else. Before she could intro-duce herself, he shrugged off his jacket, tossed it onto a chair, then returned to the stage.

After some last-minute tuning, they started playing a lively reel. It suited her mood, and apparently everyone else's. The group drew a crowd, who now stood shoulder-to-shoulder, contributing to an energy that was electric. Olivia was swept away.

When they finished the first set, the guitar player came over and asked, "What are you drinking?"

At first, she was too stunned to answer, but he stood waiting. With a glint in his eye, he glanced at his bare wrist as if checking the time. "Break's over soon."

Too charmed to decline, she said, "Dark Island."

He gave her a crooked smile that had to make most women weak in the knees. She couldn't deny its effect, and she even enjoyed it, but Olivia doubted she would ever trust him to share more than a beer. He was too smooth, which wasn't exactly a flaw. But he seemed like the sort who fell deeply in love for a day then moved on.

He returned with her beer and went back to the bar for the others. Olivia would get the next round when they finished their next set. Before the guitarist returned, Isla sat beside Olivia, followed soon by the rest of the band. After introducing Olivia as a friend of Mary McNabb, Isla went around the table with introductions. The tall violinist was Angus. Next came Fiona, who played the smallpipes and tin whistles. Ewan, the barrel-chested drummer, wasn't nearly as gruff as he looked. Last came Archie, just back with the rest of the drinks.

Isla said, "Archie, you missed the introductions. This is Olivia, a friend of your mother's."

He shook her hand and held her gaze. "Olivia, it's a pleasure to meet you. I hope my mother hasn't bored you with stories about how adorable I was as a child."

The face that followed made her laugh. "No. I didn't know she had children—"

"One child."

She continued. "Until she recommended I come see you. The group, that is. And she mentioned you."

Olivia couldn't get a read on his expression, so she added, "It was just a brief text."

"Aye, I'm sure it was, lass." Archie leaned back, arms crossed.

There was something she couldn't quite pinpoint between them. Whether friction or amusement, she couldn't tell. His lips curved in what appeared to be a smirk, hinting at some underlying tension with his mother. Was there a father figure in his life? She wasn't sure whether he was looking for sympathy or basking in his own sense of power over the moment.

Ewan eyed Archie, but it was Fiona who said, "Don't mind him. He turns on the Scots for American girls."

When the ensuing sounds of amusement subsided, Archie turned to Olivia. "Fiona's our own Miss Jean Brodie."

Olivia smiled. "I'm well past an impressionable age."

"Oh, aye, but you've made an impression on me." He leveled a deep, searching look.

With a skeptical eye, she stared back, determined to prove she was unfazed. But he was relentless. She swallowed. "What?"

Rather than answer, Archie leaned closer, his eyes searching. "Nothing," he answered quietly. Breaking the tension with a satisfied smile, he leaned back in his chair.

The conversation, which had gone on without them, turned to music. When a lull settled, Olivia seized the chance to pick their brains on some technical musical points. She asked Fiona about the difference in fingerings between the pipes and the tin whistles. Then Ewan gave her a one-minute lesson on the bodhrán. Periodically, Archie glanced toward the door.

Angus peered at him. "Are we boring you, Archie?"

"You, Angus? Never!" He glanced at Olivia. "Actually, I'm fascinated by the present company, but one of my friends was supposed to stop by." He heaved a dramatic sigh. "My first rejection of the evening. I hope there won't be a second."

Olivia couldn't shake the notion that he was referring to her.

Ewan looked at his watch. "Well, break's over. Shall we?" He stood, and the others followed his cue and took their places on the small stage. But Olivia's eyes were on Archie. With his bad-boy edge, he was hard to ignore.

She leaned back and let the music wash over her, lifting her spirits. This was the most fun she'd had since arriving in Scotland. She didn't even mind Archie's flirting, if that's what it was. It had been so long since she'd sat around a table and talked with people she liked, who made music she loved. Three songs into the set, she tore herself away to duck into the restrooms tucked away in the basement.

On her way back, she arrived at the top of the stairs and stopped. *Max?*

No doubt drawn by her tire-screeching halt, he turned and stared at her with the same stunned expression. She averted her eyes and rerouted herself as if she hadn't seen him, disappearing into the crowd near the bar.

What is he doing here? And why is he at my table? But it wasn't her table, it was the band's. That meant he must know them. Of course, he would know the musicians through his pub. *But why tonight?* Then she remembered that the band was only in town for one night.

The first thing she needed to do was abandon her seat. Finding one with a clear path to the exit would be nice—and impossible. The place was crowded enough that she could avoid him if she positioned herself behind tall people. Failing that, she could say a quick hello and escape. That could work... if she hadn't left her coat draped over her chair, beside Max. She could still sit somewhere else, and when he went to the men's room, she could grab her raincoat and flee.

It was a workable plan, but the thought of cowering in a corner in stealth mode felt silly. If he spotted her—and he would—she would look even more foolish than she already did. Moreover, it didn't seem right to miss the band that she'd come here to see over this. No, she would face things head-on.

That was when she realized Max wasn't really the problem. She was. She'd deluded herself into thinking she could control her feelings for Max. All it took was one look, and her true feelings had burst to the surface as if she'd been holding her breath underwater.

Max spotted her and made eye contact, so she smiled and went to her seat. "This is a surprise."

He looked as stunned as she'd been moments before. "You know someone in the band?"

"Not exactly. Dr. McNabb—I'm staying at her apartment—recommended the band. Her son's in it."

Max leaned back and nodded. "Of course. Archie McNabb. I know the apartment. I've been in it."

That was an unsettling thought. Max had been in her apartment? He'd have gone there with Archie, of course, before she ever arrived. So that meant Max knew Dr. McNabb. But, of course, Olivia had almost forgotten. It was Dr. McNabb who'd recommended The Red Rose to her.

Max said, "So you're staying at Mary's apartment? How did I not know this?"

Olivia shook her head. "It never came up." She glanced at the stage. "So you're friends with—"

"Archie." He nodded and stared at the table.

Still trying to piece things together, Olivia said, "So you know Dr. McNabb through Archie?"

"The reverse, actually. Our parents go way back. That's how I know Archie."

"Oh." Awkward silence followed. Olivia blamed her pounding heart. Max did that to her. He must have sensed it. Desperate to ease the tension, Olivia nodded toward the band. "Their first set was fantastic."

Max nodded.

The band started playing, so they both turned their attention to the stage. Olivia's thoughts strayed from the music. All her efforts to keep Max at bay had failed miserably. In contrast, Max seemed to have left all thoughts of her behind and was now thoroughly engrossed by the music, a fact she had ascertained by stealing glances at him.

With a sick feeling in her stomach, Olivia sighed. She had pushed him into the friend zone, and he had complied. She deserved every bit of disappointment she suffered.

Even in the midst of her misery, she couldn't help but notice the band was fantastic. This would have been an ideal evening if she were alone. Despite the circumstances, she steeled herself and fixed her attention toward the music in hope that her heightened awareness of Max would subside.

13

Max stared at the band, but his thoughts were elsewhere. Why was Olivia here, and why did it matter so much? He'd parted ways with women before. Why did she have to be different? He wanted to blame Olivia, but ending it before it could start was the logical choice. In theory. In practice, however, it wasn't, because—screw logic—he liked her. A lot. If she had to leave at the end of the semester, he would deal with that when the time came. In the meantime, they were cheating themselves of...

What? Future heartache. Olivia was right. Someone had to be sensible in this relationship that wasn't a relationship.

The band finished their set, and Olivia stood.

It seemed a little abrupt, so Max asked, "Are you leaving?"

"No, I want to buy the band a round."

That was actually a good idea, so he stood. "I'll help you."

She took in a breath as though she might protest,

but she would obviously need help getting the drinks to the table. "Okay."

Near the bar, it was too loud to talk even if they'd wanted to, so they waited in silence. Someone brushed against Max and threw him off balance.

His shoulder bumped against Olivia's. "Sorry!"

"That's okay."

Now relegated to one- and two-word phrases, they stared at the bar activity with more interest than it deserved until their drinks were ready.

"Max!" They all looked happy to see him, or it might have been the drinks. When they thanked him, he said, "Thank Olivia. This round's on her."

The table was tight to begin with, and Archie had already parked himself beside Olivia's chair, so she wound up sandwiched between Max and Archie. Max tried to ignore it, but it wasn't easy. He had known Archie for years and knew how he was around women. In Olivia's case, he couldn't really blame him. If those silky blond waves weren't enough, her eyes were a warm brown. She didn't need the soft-coral lipstick she wore. In fact, Max liked her best with no makeup. He even loved those big black glasses she wore when she was working on her laptop, especially when she looked up from the computer at him.

Archie touched Olivia's shoulder with his finger-tips. It was a simple gesture that might have been harmless coming from anyone else. If Olivia noticed, she didn't show it. She laughed and leaned forward to listen while Angus told one of his stories. Max wasn't sure how she managed it. Perhaps it was just the bond between fellow musicians, but Olivia seemed to fit in as though she'd known them for years. Unfortunately, that also went for Archie, whose arm now rested casually over the back of Olivia's chair like he owned it. Or her. It bothered Max more than it should have.

Ewan asked Max about his parents. That proved a welcome distraction until Ewan began to reminisce. He looked at Isla. "Remember the time the lad decided to sneak a wee swally?"

"Och! He couldn't have been more than six."

Ewan's eyes twinkled. "I reckon he wanted to be like the grown-ups at the pub—always drinking and chatting. So one day, when his parents weren't looking, he grabbed a pint glass and tried to pour a pint from the tap. Poor lad, he spilled beer all over himself and the floor."

Isla said, "I'm surprised you didn't stick your head under the tap."

"Don't think I wasn't tempted, but his father came over. Now that was a missed opportunity." He laughed.

Max nodded, recalling it. "He had some choice words for me—and a few chores, as well. For starters, I had to clean every inch of the bar." He leaned toward Ewan. "Don't tell my father, but my mother took pity on me and helped me."

Fiona's eyes softened. "She would. Such a kind soul."

Max nodded. He was lucky to have parents like his. He glanced over and caught Olivia's eyes, warm and shining. No matter what she said, he still felt a connection.

The evening continued, as did Archie's dogged attention to Olivia. He and Archie hardly spoke, which would have been fine, he supposed, if Archie hadn't been laser focused on Olivia. Max couldn't just sit idly by. He had to do something, so he made a preemptive move. Before the band finished their last number, Max offered to walk Olivia home.

"I was planning on calling a taxi, but a walk would be nice."

Max and Olivia said goodbye to everyone in the band except Archie. He closed his guitar case and slung it over his shoulder. Before Max could speak, Archie said, "Olivia, have you ever ridden on a motorcycle?"

She didn't answer at first, but Max was too busy glaring at Archie to notice the reason.

"No."

"Come on, then. I'll take you home."

Before Max could speak, Olivia said, "Thanks, but I've got a way home."

Archie glanced his way as Max turned to Olivia. "Ready?"

"Yes."

As Max said goodbye, he and Archie exchanged a look. They'd been friends long enough to read each other's expressions. Archie raised his eyebrows and gave Max a look that said, "Got it," and they parted ways, Archie through the back door and Max and Olivia through the front.

Outside, the watery reflections in the gutters and cracks in the cobblestone streets shimmered from a recent rain. As they walked, Max struggled to keep his thoughts to himself. He wanted to tell her how he felt, but she'd already made her feelings clear. She wanted friendship.

The walk home took about fifteen minutes, and they were mostly silent. Now and then, Max played tour guide, pointing out St. Giles' Cathedral; the Heart of Midlothian, original location of the Mercat Cross; and a couple of good pubs for music. She reacted politely but seemed preoccupied or perhaps simply tired.

When they arrived at the entrance to her building, Olivia turned to face him. "Thank you for walking me home."

"You're welcome." Max hesitated. "It was good to see you."

"It was good to see you too."

She made no move to go in, so Max said, "I'll wait till you're safely inside."

Olivia turned and touched the key fob to the sensor to unlock the door, but instead of going inside, she turned back, and the words rushed out. "Max, when I said that I wanted to be friends—"

"It's okay." It wasn't, but it seemed like the right thing to say.

She said, "I didn't know how much I'd miss you."

"You know where you can find me. Stop by anytime." It was what a friend would have said, but his voice had an edge.

Her eyes shimmered as she gazed, searching. "I'm sorry."

"Me too." A friend would have assured her it would be okay, but he couldn't lie anymore.

He didn't feel like a friend even as, with steely resolve, he tried to act like one. He didn't reach out and draw her into his arms. He didn't run his fingers through her hair, no matter how silky it looked. When his gaze fell to her lips, he didn't kiss her until neither of them could remember what had come before. Instead, he stayed still, his gaze intense and unyielding.

She whispered, "I don't want to be friends."

They flew into each other's arms, barely breathing. Her lips, soft and warm, met his. Her body moved closer to his. A slew of emotions—desire, apprehension, and joy—washed over him in waves. At that moment, he knew Olivia belonged in his arms, and he held her closer, half fearing she might change her mind. As if it were their last chance, he kissed her again.

When it ended, she whispered, "Don't let go."

They stood for a long while in each other's arms. He didn't want to leave her, so he threaded his fingers through her hair and pulled her closer.

She gently stepped back and put her hands on his chest. "I should go."

He reluctantly nodded. "Will I see you tomorrow?"

"Yes."

"Good." He slid a hand down her arm and took her hand in his. "Good night."

She squeezed his hand then let go. Once inside, she disappeared around the corner to the elevator.

Olivia. He drew in a deep breath, exhaled, and turned to walk home.

14

F or a Sunday, The Red Rose was crowded when Olivia walked into the pub.

Esme told Max, "The pressure's low on this tap." She got no response. "Max?"

Esme followed his gaze to the door, where Olivia had just stepped inside. He walked out from behind the bar to greet her.

Intrigued, Esme turned to Connor. "What's up with those two?"

Connor, having just arrived from a long shift at the hospital, looked at her, confused. She was about to explain when Max walked over and said, "Manage the bar for a couple of minutes."

Max led Olivia to her favorite table by the fire, which, Esme noticed for the first time, had a reserved sign on it. Esme leaned her elbow on the bar and watched as Max pulled out a chair for Olivia and they both sat down, starry-eyed and cozy. In the soft golden glow from the fire, their talk was quiet and unhurried.

Esme leaned closer to Connor. "When did that happen?"

"What?"

Esme muttered under her breath, "Max and Olivia."

Connor gave her a blank look. "What are you talking about?"

"Come on, Connor. Keep up." Esme shut her eyes and gave her head a slight shake. "Let me put this in terms that you'll understand. Scientifically speaking, that is what you and your lab-coat crowd would call a mating ritual."

Connor's eyes twinkled. "I think that's more anthropology than medicine, but I get your drift."

She rolled her eyes. "Whatever. My point is, Olivia looks about one step away from coyly batting her eyelashes. And Max...? He hasn't sported that happy-puppy expression since... she who shall not be named."

"Who? Paulina?" Connor's mouth quirked in the corner.

Esme leveled him with a stern look. "Did I not just say, 'she who shall not be named'?"

Connor grinned. "You're a little high-strung tonight. You might need a break from that bar."

"Tell me about it." She smirked and fixed her attention on Max, who tenderly smoothed a strand of Olivia's hair from her face.

Esme sighed. "I've a sudden craving for a languid puff on a cigarette and an evening with Charles Boyer."

Connor wrinkled his face in confusion. "I didn't know you smoked."

Esme's eyes shone. "I don't. They just look so romantic."

"I don't get the connection with cigarettes."

"*Now, Voyager*. Classic film. They didn't have sex scenes back then, so they smoked cigarettes."

"You've lost me. So you want to have sex?"

"No!" Esme froze. "No... No, that's not what I meant!"

"I didn't mean with me. I just meant—"

"No, of course not." She couldn't bring herself to look at him. "Because that would be..."

"Right." With a nod, Connor stared at his drink. "Simple misunderstanding."

Esme forced herself to stop nodding. "It's just me being a classic film nerd." Feeling her face getting hot and red, she escaped to the other end of the bar on the pretense of working.

With a kiss on the forehead, Max left Olivia and returned to the bar, looking blissful. Meanwhile, Esme was one step away from breathing into a paper bag. The best thing was to pretend her conversation with Connor had never happened. Max was the perfect diversion.

While Max managed the opposite end of the bar, Olivia took a seat at the bar beside Connor. "It looks like we're on our own here."

Connor stared at his drink. "I'm used to it."

When she'd regained her composure, Esme's curiosity drove her to Olivia to get the full story about Max. "So... what's up with you two?"

"Who? Max and me? Nothing. We're friends."

Esme frowned skeptically. "Friends who kiss?"

Olivia's jaw dropped, but she couldn't seem to protest.

Esme beamed victoriously.

Olivia rolled her eyes and heaved a sigh. "Okay,

fine! When Noah and I broke up, I made two resolutions: don't look back and don't fall in love. Now look at me."

Esme lifted an eyebrow. "I am."

"What?"

Esme folded her arms. "You as much as said you're in love with Max."

Olivia grew defensive. "I did not. I never mentioned the *L* word—at least not in reference to anyone here."

Esme's eyes twinkled mischievously. "Oh, so you've fallen in love with some random guy—*not* here?"

"No, because I'm going home at the end of the semester."

Esme nodded. "Right, and it's impossible to fall in love during a semester."

Olivia thought for a moment. "No. I think it's one of those weird laws you have here in Scotland—like you can't fish for salmon on a Sunday, and you can't fall in love midsemester."

Esme lifted her chin in a slow nod. "That's right. It dates back to the early Edinburgh University days when American women kept coming over to Scotland and falling in love with our lads."

Olivia wrinkled her face. "In 1582? Because that's when it was founded."

"Sure. It's the accents and kilts. You lot can't help yourselves."

"Oh. Well, you might have a point." It was futile to pretend anymore.

Esme scooted her chair forward. "What's going on? Tell me everything."

Olivia was beaming. "There's not much to tell. I guess we both gave up trying to fight it."

Esme said, "Girl, I've been on team Olivia from the start, so I'm happy for you—and for Max."

Olivia's expression clouded over. "I just can't let myself think about the end of the semester."

Esme reflected. "Maybe it doesn't have to end."

Olivia shook her head slowly. "It will, and then I'll go home, and Max will stay here."

Esme tried but couldn't think of a positive spin.

Olivia shrugged. "Which is why it would've been easier if we'd kept our distance. Believe me, I tried. But Max is just..."

Esme's eyes softened. "Hard not to like."

Olivia's eyes widened. "Exactly. Oh. I didn't even think that you..."

"Me?" Esme shook her head emphatically. "No! I didn't mean to imply... No, Max and I are just friends." She stole a glance at Connor. "Max and I are like brother and sister, in all the best and worst ways. When we're not looking out for each other, we bicker and drive each other mad." Even as she laughed, she felt uncomfortable in Connor's presence. This ridiculous crush had a way of making normal moments feel awkward.

Eager to change the subject, she turned to Olivia. "So, tell me about Scottish traditional folk music."

Olivia laughed at the abrupt change of subjects. "I don't think I can tell you anything you don't already know."

Esme didn't quite buy that. "I doubt that. But what interests me is why you're studying it."

Olivia looked away with an embarrassed expression. "Oh, you know. The Scottish ancestry thing was a big part of it, which you must hear all the time."

Esme smiled politely. "Just a wee bit. Americans, Canadians, Australians... I could go on. Your ancestors must've done a really hard sell on Scotland."

"Are you kidding? Look around you! Who wouldn't miss all this?"

"You haven't even been to the Highlands yet, have you?" Esme smiled knowingly.

Max popped into the conversation on his way to grab a lime wedge from the counter. "We'll have to remedy that."

Esme said, "That sounds like date number one."

Max looked at Olivia. "Plan on it."

She nodded.

Esme delivered a pint to a customer at the end of the bar then returned to pick up where they'd left off. "You were saying that your ancestry was one reason to study folk music. What was the other?"

Olivia drew in a quick breath. "Oh, right. Besides that, I majored in voice, so studying folk songs seemed like an obvious choice."

"That's right. You're a singer. We'll have to put you to work!"

Olivia shook her head. "Oh, no. I stopped singing when I got busy teaching and working on my dissertation. I'm so out of shape now, I don't know what would come out if I tried."

"A Scottish song, I hope. Do you know any? Of course you must. You're studying them."

"Yes, but—"

A mischievous twinkle lit Esme's eyes. "All I heard was yes." She looked at Connor and raised her eyebrows, hinting for him to agree.

It took him a moment, but he chimed in. "Aye."

Before Olivia could protest, the musicians started playing. Music soared over the pub noise.

Under the guise of having work to do, Esme disappeared, only to reappear on the stage, mic in hand. "We have in our presence a singer. If you lot will be nice, we might coax a song out of her. Let's hear it for Olivia!" Esme started the applause then held out the mic.

After an encouraging nudge from Connor, Olivia went to the stage. The only person more surprised than Olivia was Max, who stopped in his tracks and stood transfixed.

Ignoring Olivia's panicked face, Esme stepped down from the stage and returned to the bar. After a quick conversation among the musicians, a ballad began, and Olivia sang.

> *I know where I'm going,*
> > *And I know who's going with me,*
> > *I know who I love,*
> > *But the dear knows who I'll marry...*

THE CONVERSATIONS STOPPED, and the room grew quiet as Olivia's sweet soprano filled the room. Time slowed down while her words floated over the crowd, captivating everyone in the room.

Max stopped serving drinks, got his fiddle, and joined her. Even Esme and Connor fell silent, spellbound by the ethereal strains. Too soon, Olivia's last note hung in the air, suspended for a moment. The room slowly came back to life, and the crowd burst into applause. Max and Olivia smiled at each other, and Max whispered something in her ear. She blushed and nodded, and they left the stage.

OLIVIA ESCAPED through the doors to the kitchen to regain her composure. By some miracle, most likely adrenaline, her voice had come through, despite her lack of practice. She'd nearly forgotten how terrifying yet wonderful it felt to sing. She felt a strong sense of having joined a centuries-long series of musicians, each offering their unique interpretation and love of the music.

Startled by the sound of the swinging doors, Olivia turned to find Max with a smile that lit the room and warmed her heart.

Slowly, he shook his head. "I didn't know."

Still soaring from the joy of singing again, she couldn't form the words to reply.

Full of awe, he said, "You can sing." His eyes widened with admiration as he walked slowly toward her and took her hands in his.

Olivia gazed into his eyes. "You might be a little biased." But when she sang in this historic pub, she felt something she'd never known before. It went beyond her love of music to a sense of the history and tradition behind the songs. The lyrics represented people's lives and their stories. Now she was a part of it, and she felt whole.

If the joy of singing had gone to her head and was clouding her judgment, she didn't care. Max drew her into his arms and kissed her with stunning intensity. As each kiss bound them closer together, she knew this was where she belonged. After months adrift with no family, she'd found a place to call home. She silenced the voice that reminded her it couldn't last. She was in Max's arms, and she would cling to this moment.

Esme's voice cut into her dream. "Oh!"

Startled, Max and Olivia separated then smiled, embarrassed.

Without making eye contact, Esme pointed to a shelf. "Erm... I'll just grab that bottle and go." She pointed back toward the door, as if words weren't enough. "Got it. As you were. This is me leaving." She grabbed the bottle and quickly left through the swinging doors.

Max said, "You heard what she said. As we were."

Olivia was still laughing when he kissed her again, but her laughter soon faded. It felt right to be with him. She stopped thinking and reveled in the feel of his lips against hers, his arms about her, and his body against hers. It didn't matter where he ended and she began, because, even if just for a moment, they belonged together.

Max broke away, his eyes warm with desire. "If we don't go back out there, I'll be tempted to sweep you into my arms and take you upstairs."

"I'd be tempted to let you."

He stepped back, looking solemn. "I think we both know that would be a mistake."

Her emotions were so out of control, she didn't want to hear it. She wanted Max even if it would break her heart later.

He said, "There would be no turning back."

Olivia heaved a sigh. "I know." She searched his

eyes, hoping he would whisk her upstairs to his bed, but there was too much at stake. Sleeping together would be incredible and heartbreaking.

Then Max surprised her and took the decision from her. Clasping her hand, he led her back to the pub. Their favorite table was taken, so they joined Connor at the end of the bar.

Connor smiled at her. "That was beautiful."

"Thanks." She had never gotten used to people's reactions to her singing, but she always appreciated it.

While Max and Connor talked football, Olivia reflected. Max was right. They'd just dodged a heart-breaking mistake.

Esme set down two pints for some patrons then joined them. "That was gorgeous! Of course, now you're signed up as a regular."

Olivia shook her head, laughing.

As the night advanced, the pub emptied, so Esme urged Max and Olivia to leave. Connor even offered to help Esme close up.

Taking them up on their offer, Max and Olivia left and strolled, hands entwined, into the chilly Edinburgh night.

15

E sme handed a wet bar towel to Connor, her eyes full of doubt. "Are you sure about this? I'm fine cleaning up by myself. It's not like I haven't done it a million times before."

"But not with me. Let me help." He rolled up his sleeves and got busy.

As Esme worked, she said, "I still can't get over those two and their instant transformation. One day, they're just friends, then the next day they're... not just friends."

Connor finished wiping down the bar and paused for a moment. "The heart is a powerful muscular organ."

Esme stopped and peered at him. "You sure know how to sweet-talk a girl!"

"Hence my success with the ladies."

Esme placed the last chair upside down on a table. Then she poured two glasses of Drambuie and handed one to Connor. "Have a seat. Here's a nightcap—or wages."

She sat beside him. "So... since you brought it up, how's the dating life going?"

He stared at her with narrowing eyes. "Do you really want to know?"

"I wouldn't have asked if I didn't."

He heaved a sigh. "Well... I went out with this woman..." He rolled his eyes. "She was too in love with her phone to bother with me. It was impressive how much she could talk and scroll through her phone at the same time. She had so much screen time during our date that I'm convinced she wouldn't recognize me if she saw me again."

Esme winced but was secretly pleased then guilty about it. Each dating failure gave her more hope.

"The next date was the opposite. Total silence."

"She didn't talk at all?"

Connor shook his head. "Believe me, I tried to draw her out. I used my bedside manner technique—not literally. Conversationally." His eyebrows furrowed. "You know what I mean."

Esme nodded, unable to hide her amusement.

Connor looked off into the distance. "She was painfully shy. I felt sorry for her, but with her shyness and my being..." He helplessly lifted his palms. "You know... me. We faced a hopeless future of being crossed off everyone's cocktail party list. Not that I really go to cocktail parties, but..."

"Just not a good fit."

"Exactly." Connor frowned.

He was mulling something over. Esme hoped it was her. But that was always the hope every time she was with him, so she did her best to look positive.

"Okay. The thing is... sometimes I can laugh about

these when they're over, but this next one was just weird. We met at a restaurant in New Town. She looked even better than her picture, and she seemed really nice." He paused, looking troubled. "They always seem nice at first. We sat down, placed our orders. So far, so good. Then I asked her about her interests and hobbies. She listed them, sounding almost rehearsed. Mystery novels, politics, and the paranormal. I was thinking maybe a ghost hunter show or some sort of ancient mystery documentary."

Esme nodded. "Nothing wrong with that."

"No, it was fine. There was a lull in the conversation, and we happened to be seated by a window. I looked out and, to fill in the silence, commented that it looked like a full moon."

Esme nodded, approving. "Great topic! Very romantic."

"One would think, but she practically slammed her palms on the table, leaned forward wild-eyed, and whispered, 'The moon landing was fake.'"

Esme rolled her eyes. "Why is it always the moon landing?" She shook her head and leaned back. "So, what did you say?"

"Nothing. I was too busy choking on my haggis."

Esme's eyes widened. "I'll bet that made an impression."

"Of sorts. But she must've mistaken my shocked disbelief for interest, because she proceeded to explain, in far more detail than I'll share with you now, that the American government staged it to make it seem like they'd won the space race, when it was really—"

"The Russians."

"Aliens."

Confused, Esme wrinkled her face. "But... wouldn't the aliens, kind of by definition, already have won the space race?"

Connor tilted his head. "Yes. There were one or two gaping holes in her theory, but I let it go. She went on to explain it was all simulated using computer-generated imagery."

"Wait! Don't tell me Michael Jackson's moonwalk wasn't real either!"

"Go on, laugh. But at the time, it wasn't so funny."

"Sorry." Esme tried to look contrite. "What do you say to something like that?"

"I said, 'Read any good books lately?'"

"Connor, maybe your dating app's algorithm needs a little tweaking."

"A little tweaking? It needs a race car pit crew to change the tires, rebuild the engine, and send me on my way."

Esme pouted sincerely. "Poor you."

Connor took a sip of his drink. "In retrospect, I should've said I was sick or pretended to get called into the hospital for an emergency. But it seemed rude, even mean, so I couldn't."

"Because you're so nice."

"Or daft." Connor sighed. "So I hung in there through her theory about chemtrails. Did you know a foreign government is using balloons to spray chemicals into the air so we'll all breathe them in?"

Esme didn't believe it any more than Connor did, but now she was curious. "Why?"

"To make us all docile, so we'll comply with their wishes."

"Which government?"

"I didn't ask. China? Canada?"

Bright-eyed, Esme nodded. "It's part of the Great Reset!"

He laughed. "I managed to shift the topic to a relatively normal conversation about house pets and wildlife." With a pleasant smile, Connor added, "And lizard people."

"Oh!" Esme burst into laughter, and Connor joined in.

When they calmed down, Connor said, "Thank God the topic of lizard people came up over dessert, so the end was near." He leaned closer, lifted an eyebrow, and lowered his voice. "There's an elite force of them gaining a foothold in the British government. They're half human—the top half, so you can't really tell. Although, you'll never see them near a swimming pool. The webbed feet are a dead giveaway." He nodded knowingly.

Esme was beyond laughter now. "Okay. So forget tweaking that dating app. Just delete it."

Connor looked surprised. "Did you think that's the only app I've used? Oh, no. I've tried them all."

Esme rested her chin in her hand. "Maybe you should try a different strategy."

"Like what?"

She hesitated. "People you meet in real life." She feared she'd gone too far, but he didn't seem to relate it to her.

Connor said, "The only people I meet in real life are patients, and, of course, other doctors. But there's no one at work I'd be interested in. Besides, with my luck, I'd ask someone out on a date and get slapped with a sexual harassment complaint."

Esme considered pointing out that he was in The Red Rose at least once a week, sometimes twice. He could meet someone here—for example, a bonny bartender named Esme, who was more or less normal and would love to go out with him.

Connor looked at his watch. "Sorry, I didn't realize how late it was." He stood and put on his coat. "So that's my sad story. Next time, I want to hear yours."

"Sure. Next time."

Esme slipped on her jacket, and they walked out into the chilly night air.

After Esme locked up, Connor said, "It's late. I'll walk you home."

"You don't have to. I'm just around the block."

With a cheery shrug, he said, "It's no trouble."

She couldn't argue. He was making eye contact, and she always got stupid when he did that. "Okay." So they walked down the street while Esme silently formed her own conspiracy theory about the invisible force field that seemed to emanate from her.

16

Early Tuesday morning, Max picked Olivia up at her apartment and, after stopping to stock up on coffee and snacks, headed north to the Highlands. He made the journey even more enjoyable by sharing his stories about the landmarks they passed. Olivia was so captivated that by the time they arrived at his parents' house, she felt like she'd learned enough about the area to become a tour guide. She was particularly taken by the glistening Loch Lomond, but she'd always found water soothing. It didn't matter whether it was a lake—or loch, as they called them in Scotland—or the sea. She loved it all.

They stepped out of the car and climbed the steps to his parents' refurbished croft. With a deep breath, Max paused at the entrance and knocked. His father, Malcolm, greeted them with kind eyes and a face visibly unscathed by the stroke he'd suffered. Max's mother, Rhona, welcomed them into the cozy kitchen. Aromas of freshly baked scones, clotted cream, and jam filled the room.

Olivia took an immediate liking to Rhona, and it seemed to be mutual. As they sat in the snug, sipping tea, Rhona said, "You must come back for Christmas. Summer is all about tourists, but Christmas is about a brisk walk along a snow-dusted path. Then you duck into a cozy neighborhood pub for a warming drink, a seat by the fire, and good *craic*."

"Craic?"

Rhona's eyes twinkled. "Conversation with your neighbors and friends."

"That sounds... magical. Where I'm from, there's nothing quite like the Highlands, but we have some spectacular waterfalls. In the dead of winter, the cascading water freezes, making it look like time has stopped. It's one of my favorite places, although the Scottish Highlands might bump it down a notch on the list."

After enjoying his mother's delicious baked treats, she and Max headed out for their tour of the Highlands. They spent their day exploring by car and on foot, walking hand in hand, or stopping to picnic at a riverbank in between hikes in the hills, taking photos at a castle ruin.

The roads wound through dense woods and quaint country villages, and they even caught sight of a towering castle in the distance. They toured the grounds of one castle ruin, exploring what was left of its many rooms and chambers. Max regaled Olivia with stories of battles fought long ago and of generations of kings who had lived here.

From there, they headed north. Rolling hills dotted with sheep gave way to dramatic mountains and valleys. Max stopped for Olivia's photo ops, complete with arm-in-arm selfies. Large swaths of the Highlands were tree-less, but they drove past wooded patches with leaves just beginning to turn into their autumn colors. A deep sense of wonder settled over Olivia.

By late afternoon, losing daylight, they returned to his parents' house. At Rhona's insistence, they stayed for the best meal Olivia had eaten since arriving in Scotland. Malcolm recalled his favorite hiking trails, which he dreamed of revisiting someday.

Max clasped Olivia's hand. "Come out to the garden. Let's look at the stars."

The sight outside was breathtaking. It was an uncharacteristically clear October night, and the stars twinkled brightly against a black-velvet sky. "Max, it's stunning."

He slipped his hand into hers. "Aye, it is that. The pub keeps me so busy, I'm not able to come here enough."

Olivia was puzzled. "How did your parents do it when you were younger?"

"Oh, we didn't live here. We all lived in the apartment above the pub. This was my grandparents' place. They moved here after my parents took over the pub, so this was like a second home. I spent a lot of time here with my grandparents, and we all spent our holidays here."

"How wonderful for you."

"It was—and it is."

Olivia gazed at Max, and her heart filled with affection. "Thank you for bringing me here."

"I wanted to show you the Scotland I love." Max smiled, and they stood in comfortable silence.

After a warm goodbye, Max and Olivia headed

back to Edinburgh. The Rover's standard transmission did not deter Max from holding Olivia's hand when he could. It was late when he dropped her off at her apartment with a kiss and whispered goodbye. As her elevator door closed, Olivia heaved a sigh. She had fallen in love with the Highlands and the sense of belonging she'd felt with his parents. Not that she truly belonged, but for a few hours, they made her feel like she was part of a family—Max's family.

Max. She sighed. If she wasn't careful, she might fall in love.

Maybe she already had.

THE NEXT DAY WAS A WORKDAY. Olivia vowed not to let thoughts of Max interfere with her work. She had traveled too far to salvage this project to let it fail now.

The rain wouldn't let up. Olivia stood at the window. On the sidewalk below, people walked by in hooded raincoats. Most seemed to have abandoned their umbrellas, which were useless against the driving rain and wind gusts. She decided it was a sign that she should stay home to work. Minutes later, she settled down at the table with a wall of windows before her and a cup of coffee beside her, poised to meet the day's goals.

Throughout the morning, she sailed through long patches of intense productivity, pausing only to refill her coffee. Then her mind would wander to Max. She would recall something he'd said or a place they had seen, and twenty minutes would pass before she came to her senses. After one such lapse, she'd just gotten back on course when her phone dinged with a text message from Max.

Max: *I miss you. Do you ever get time off for good behavior?*

Olivia: *Sadly, no—not unless I reach my goal for the day.*

Max: *You know, there's an art to goal setting. They should be specific, measurable, and—this part is key—achievable.*

Olivia: *Really? And how does texting fit into it?*

Max: *Are you suggesting I'm a bad influence?*

Olivia: *Not in so many words.*

Max: *Oh.*

Olivia: *But I miss you too... So let me get back to work so I can finish.*

Max: *And come see me tonight?*

Olivia: *Yes... If I get my work done.*

Max: *Good. See you later!*

Olivia: *Fingers crossed!*

SHE MET Max that night and the next. While he slept in from a late night at work, she would work through the morning. Around lunchtime, they would spend a few hours together exploring the city then part ways for a few hours while Olivia worked. Then, unless she was going to hear live music elsewhere, she would join him at the pub. There, she would sit at a corner table and listen, at times taking notes. The music was never the same but almost always inspiring. She had never been so productive.

One afternoon, Max suggested they take a day off

and spend it together exploring Edinburgh. Olivia was due for a break, so they set off early and stopped for breakfast at a cozy café just off the Royal Mile. The weather was typical October weather, drizzly and windy, but they didn't care. They walked past several Royal Mile landmarks then ducked into St. Giles Cathedral. Stopping at each alcove, Max would entertain Olivia with stories and anecdotes. The Thistle Chapel was her favorite, steeped in tradition that dated back to the Middle Ages. They revisited the National Museum of Scotland, which offered new discoveries with each visit.

After a twilight wander through Princes Street Gardens, they found their way to a cozy little music pub on Rose Street. Live music and laughter drew them inside, where they dried off and warmed up.

Max set down his empty glass. "Let's go grab a bite."

"Yes!" Olivia pulled on her raincoat, and they left.

Princes Street was still bustling when they crossed it and headed up the North Bridge to Old Town. Max led the way to a cozy little restaurant on the Royal Mile, where he had haggis, while Olivia opted for fresh-grilled salmon and mash. Beneath the soft glow of fairy lights and candles, they shared stories about their very different lives. Olivia had never been so completely content.

It was dark when they walked along the cobbled sidewalks, dodging strays from meandering ghost tours and pub crawls. They arrived at Olivia's flat. She fished her key fob from her pocket. "What a perfect day!"

Max wrapped his arms around her and kissed her.

He whispered, "The only thing better than spending the day with you would be spending the night."

Olivia closed her eyes and sighed. "I know…"

Before she could finish the thought, he brushed his lips against hers and kissed her deeply. It nearly swept her away. With what little willpower she had left, she resisted. "It'll just make it worse."

Saying nothing, he just leaned his forehead on hers and heaved a deep sigh. He stepped back and kissed her forehead. "Goodnight."

His mood shifted so quickly, she wasn't sure how to react.

"Max, I'm sorry."

He turned back long enough to say, "Don't be." Then he disappeared around the corner.

Once upstairs, Olivia stewed about Max while she got ready for bed. After a perfect day, their parting was not. What little they said had an undercurrent of unexpressed emotions, not to mention desire. Did he think she didn't want him as much as he wanted her? Had he kissed her and held her again, she might have led him by the hand to her flat. They would have had the sort of head-exploding passion that made fireworks pale in comparison. She was certain of it.

That was the one thing that kept her from sleeping with him. Once they did, she would be so deeply in love and so entirely vulnerable that leaving him would destroy her. She was practically there already—a hair's breadth from falling hopelessly in love. But the truth loomed before her. She was going to leave him, and that made her wonder. How completely could a heart shatter before there were no pieces left to pick up?

17

Max and Olivia cherished their time together, increasingly so as the end of the semester drew near. A few nights a week, Max would take an hour's break to hear music at nearby pubs. On his few evenings off, they explored the city together, sampling restaurants and live music and soaking up the unique culture of Edinburgh.

One night, they walked into a small pub on the outskirts of Old Town. The warm air was heavy with ale and acoustic music. A small table opened near the musicians, so they sat side by side with their backs to the wall. Olivia typed away at her laptop while Max watched her and, occasionally, the musicians. As the night progressed, the music quieted down to a plaintive ballad.

When Olivia closed her laptop to listen, Max leaned closer and whispered, "I'm falling in love with you."

Olivia couldn't breathe for a moment.

Concerned by her reaction, Max said, "I'm sorry. That was blunt."

She could barely speak, but once she started, the words poured out. "We weren't going to get serious. It was our understanding. We both know how it is. There's no future." She looked about. There were so many people. "I need some air."

She grabbed her jacket and rushed outside, only to find herself next to a couple of men on a smoke break. She took a few steps away from the smoke. Seconds later, Max caught up with her, laptop bag slung over his shoulder, and fell into step. The cool mist in the night air felt good on her face.

Halfway down the block, Max said, "I handled that well, don't you think?" He let out an exasperated sound. "Look, I'm an eejit, but I—"

A young guy, clearly under the influence, rounded the corner and staggered into Max. He grabbed Max's shoulders to keep from falling, and Max steadied him. He gave the guy a pat on the back. "You okay, mate?"

He turned unfocused eyes toward Max. "Aye," he said and ambled down the sidewalk.

"Och!" Max clutched his pocket and cursed.

Alarmed, Olivia asked, "What's wrong?"

"That lad got my wallet."

"Oh, no!"

"It's okay. It was only my mugger's wallet. I'm just angry that I let him get away with it."

"Was there very much money in it?"

Still angry with himself, Max rolled his eyes. "A couple of tenners, but he didn't get my ID or credit cards."

Max put his arm around Olivia's waist. "Come on. Let's go somewhere quiet and talk."

"It's late. Isn't everything closed?"

"I know a place."

Ordinarily, she might have put him off until tomorrow, when clearer heads would prevail, but the pickpocket incident had shaken her up. At the moment, all she wanted was to be somewhere safe with Max. Her heart, not her head, was driving her, but his earlier confession had thrown her off-balance.

When Max led her down the alley just before The Red Rose, Olivia eyed him with suspicion. "When you said you knew a place, I assumed you meant a late-night café."

"They're all closed."

"Yeah, so I gather."

He stopped and turned to her. "I just want to talk. I promise I'll be a perfect gentleman."

"I know you will." Olivia hesitated. "It's just that..." She couldn't tell him the truth—that it wasn't a question of his being a gentleman. She didn't trust herself. If she could just keep her distance, then saying goodbye wouldn't hurt as much. She now realized that was a lie she'd been telling herself. He was right. "I guess we do need to talk."

They climbed the stairs to his flat. In all the time she'd known him, they'd never been to each other's apartments. She wasn't sure what she'd imagined his apartment would look like, but it wasn't this. Tall casement windows lined the back wall. She walked over and peered out the window, where a breathtaking view of Edinburgh Castle loomed large in the distance. From its perch atop ancient volcanic rock, warm amber light bathed its rough stone walls.

"You wake up to this every day?"

Max smiled.

Olivia tore herself from the window and took in the flat, with its vaulted ceiling of cream-colored plaster held up by sturdy wooden beams. The windows were flanked by tartan drapes, and a matching tartan rug covered most of the dark wood floor. A small black wood stove sat nestled into a corner, flanked by two comfortable-looking leather chairs. The sofa and remaining side pieces were eclectic and yet all looked charming together. Other than a jacket slung over a chair back and a couple of paperbacks on the coffee table, it could have been a photo from a vacation rental website.

"It's so cozy!"

"Don't look at me. This is all my mother's work. Although I should add that I made a few adjustments after they moved to the Highlands. I have no complaints. It's been perfect for me."

"She's done a great job." It exuded such warmth and comfort that Olivia had no trouble imagining herself spending time here. That just made matters worse. Max was becoming impossible to resist.

As they stood in the middle of the room, a silence descended upon them, a reminder of why they'd come here. Since arriving, their talk had been pleasant and light, but a serious conversation waited, making the tension between them palpable.

He gestured for her to take a seat on the sofa, then he sat on the opposite end. "When I said... what I said, I spoke out of turn. Please don't let this change things between us."

She said softly, "How can it not?"

He looked down, frowning. "I don't want to lose what we've got."

She felt helpless. "What have we got? I don't know what that is anymore."

"We're friends."

"Friends who love each other."

He lifted his eyes to meet hers. "Did you just say...?"

She shut her eyes for a moment and sighed. "Yes." She wished she could feel as happy as he looked, but she felt quite the opposite. "We're friends who love each other—who can't be together."

Max looked away as though he weren't even talking to her. "Why can't love be enough?" Gazing at her with such love in his eyes only made matters worse.

"Geography? Work? We should never have met."

He looked bitterly wounded. "Is that what you wish?"

"No! That's not what I meant!" She reached for his hand, but he rose and went to the window.

He was shutting her out. She couldn't blame him. For weeks, he'd been there beside her, even when she kept him at arm's length. But now, he was the one putting distance between them, and it hurt. All the heartache she'd tried to insulate herself from came crashing in from all sides. She hadn't controlled her feelings or prevented any pain.

She said softly, "I've been such a fool." She hadn't meant it for Max, but he heard her.

"Why?"

"Because I tried not to love you."

He turned from the window. "I didn't. I just loved you—almost from the start."

Olivia was so weary of working against her emotions. She wanted Max to ignore everything that she said, whisk her into his arms, and make her forget everything in their way. But he stood by the window, and he wouldn't move—not one step toward her.

The next moment, without thinking, she stood and went to him, but he wouldn't turn from the window. She put her hand on his shoulder. "Max, please."

"Please what? You seem to have made up your mind. I respect that. But don't ask me to be happy about it."

"I'm not. I just..."

He turned toward her but avoided eye contact, then he looked back at the castle.

She continued. "I don't want to lose you."

He cast a burning look at her. "But you will." The words caught in his throat. "Because love is not enough."

His words dealt a harsh blow. None of this fit what she'd planned for her life, because she'd never planned to meet Max. "I'm in love with you too."

She barely got the words out before he drew her to him, and she buried her face in his chest. Max tilted her chin up and kissed her softly and tentatively. As it deepened, Olivia wrapped her arms around Max's neck, pulling him closer as he slid his hand up her back.

He held her and whispered, "I love you," then he kissed her again.

They broke away, and their eyes locked. Mixed emotions flowed freely—desire, disbelief, and elation.

Then Olivia kissed him. It was too late for everything now—too late to be friends, to avoid falling in love, and to protect their hearts.

Max pulled away, took a deep breath, and exhaled. "Either I walk you home... or into that bedroom. Tell me which."

She glanced toward the bedroom. "I want to... I'd better... go home."

As he nodded, a warm light came to his eyes. "Let's go."

They walked arm in arm, sometimes stopping to kiss, other times talking quietly, but neither mentioned the future.

18

A cool wind tossed the leaves about on a gray afternoon as, inside The Red Rose, Olivia closed her laptop and stared blankly through the window.

Max sauntered over to her. "Are you all right? You look like you've seen a ghost."

She looked up, dazed. "I'm done."

He looked at her empty coffee cup. "If you're tired, I can get you more coffee."

She shook her head slowly. "I don't need it. I'm done. Max, I've finished my dissertation." Light slowly came to her eyes as she leaned back in her chair. "I can hardly believe it."

He smiled, but it didn't reach his eyes. "Congratulations." It was the right thing to say, but it took obvious effort. His face brightened. "Wait here." He bounded over to the bar, grabbed a bottle of champagne and three glasses, and returned with Esme. When everyone had a glass, he lifted his. "Here's to the future Dr. Olivia Boyd!"

Connor walked into the pub in time for Esme to grab one more glass and draw him into the festivities.

Esme exclaimed, "We need music!"

She and Connor moved to the bar and leaned over her phone to find a sufficiently celebratory playlist to play over the sound system. At least, that was Esme's excuse. Olivia suspected she wanted to give them a moment alone, prompting Olivia to wonder whether Max had said something to her. Not that it was necessary. If Olivia had picked up on Max's clouded expression, Esme might have too. Either way, it didn't take any mystical Scottish second sight to discern what was wrong. With her work done, she would be leaving. But they'd always known that. Any time they'd had together was borrowed.

She wouldn't think of that now. Olivia sipped her champagne, determined to revel in her moment of victory. "I can hardly believe it! Of course, it's a draft. I just uploaded it to my professor, so we'll see what she says. I'm sure there'll be changes—loads of changes."

But there weren't. Two days later, her advisor emailed. It was glowing. Her hunch had been right. Coming to Scotland had transformed Olivia's dissertation. She went on about how immersing herself in the music and hearing it played in historic locations had breathed life into Olivia's work. But the last part of the email caught Olivia entirely off guard. "Of course, it'll need to be proofread, but other than that, I wouldn't change a thing."

"'I wouldn't change a thing.'" Olivia echoed the words with disbelief as she leaned back in her chair and stared out the window at the hills in the distance, now capped white from a recent snowstorm. She wondered how many times she'd looked up from her work at those hills that had brought her small moments of peace. So often, she'd dreamed of this moment. But now, the sad truth of it gripped her. That familiar view and the Scotland she'd come to adore would soon be a memory. She loved it so deeply. And Max. She'd be leaving him too. Tamping down the thought, she closed her laptop and got up, determined to enjoy her last days in Scotland.

But the last day came too soon.

OLIVIA PUSHED OPEN the door to The Red Rose pub. The warm, wood-fire-scented air hit her as she stepped inside. The amber glow of the pub washed over her with a comfort she desperately longed to remember when she was back home.

Connor was there in his usual place, so Olivia joined him. "What's going on? I've never seen it like this on a Wednesday."

Connor smirked. "Yeah, I came here for a quiet drink after work." He rolled his eyes. "It's a bus tour from the hotel down the street. Retired librarians. Americans. Wild bunch." He tilted his head toward an animated conversation and laughter in progress at a table nearby.

Esme arrived with Olivia's usual half-pint.

Olivia lifted her glass. "Thank you!"

Esme waved it off. "Max is trapped, but he'll be down in a minute."

At the opposite end of the bar, Max was leaning on the bar, sleeves rolled up to reveal his brawny forearms. He shook his head toward two young women. As if reading her mind, he glanced over and grinned. Despite the countless hours they'd spent together, one look could send indescribable warmth through her. No man would ever make her feel like that again.

After freeing himself, he walked to her and leaned over the bar to whisper in her ear. "You look lovely. If it weren't for all these people, I'd kiss you right now." He leaned back and looked into her eyes so deeply, if she hadn't been seated, her knees would have buckled.

"You're busy."

"Not too busy for you."

Connor cleared his throat loudly, as if to remind them of his presence.

Max turned to Connor. "We've got a couple of students who are getting a bit too rowdy for my liking. I just cut them off and called a taxi."

A loud thud brought a hush to the room. Max cursed under his breath. One woman fell off her bar stool, and the other was laughing too hard to pull her up to her feet.

Taking a moment to sigh and run a hand through his hair, he said, "Excuse me," then went to their aid.

Olivia watched as Max deftly guided the two women to their waiting cab. One leaned against him and ran her hand down his shoulder and upper arm. "I love a man with a mus... sc... scular-r arm."

Connor said, "That's easy for you to say."

The second woman, glued to his other side, was kept afloat by Max's other apparently muscular arm.

Olivia wanted to laugh, but she couldn't take her eyes off Max as he peeled the women from either side and eventually deposited them in a taxi.

Connor leaned back, entertained. "They're a bit like human barnacles, don't you think?"

Olivia considered the concept.

Max returned, shaking his head. "Sorry about that. I only served them two drinks. Clearly, this wasn't their first stop."

Olivia nodded. "You handled it well."

Max's eyes crinkled at the corners. "Thank you. So, how was your day?"

"Good." She didn't mention that, despite her reluctance, she was quickly tying up the loose ends. She avoided the topic as if talking about it would make it more real.

"I'm glad." And he was. She could see it in his eyes, but she also saw in his wistful expression the same conflicting emotions she'd been battling all day. He leaned across the bar and kissed her. "You should celebrate."

She laughed. "I've been celebrating for a couple of days now! If I celebrate any more, I'll be like your two friends who just left."

With a crooked grin that always made her heart flutter, he handed her a half-pint. "I promise I won't overserve you."

Even as she smiled in response, a wave of melancholy spread through her heart. She wondered if this was how it would be from now on, with her trying to cling to each moment, look, and smile because it was one of the last. Forcing herself to turn from those thoughts, she took a sip of her drink.

A commotion erupted at the end of the bar. Esme was trying to calm down a customer.

Max heaved a weary sigh. "That's just Frank. There must be a full moon tonight."

Olivia watched as Max made his way over to Esme and Frank, her heart pounding with worry. She had seen Frank before but never paid much attention to him. Max casually leaned on both hands and spoke to him in a calm, measured tone. It worked wonders. Judging from their body language, the tension had eased.

Olivia relaxed. "He's really good at that." She hadn't meant to say it out loud, but Connor heard and agreed.

When Max returned, Olivia regarded him with newfound respect. "How do you do it?"

With a shrug, he said, "It's part of the job. I've been trained by the best—years of watching my father and grandfather."

Olivia took another sip of her drink. "But you make it look easy."

Max fixed his eyes on her. "The world might conspire against us, but I won't let it ruin our evening."

Esme was suddenly there, although Olivia couldn't have said when she had joined them. "I'll ask the musicians to play something calming."

"What we need is a song," Connor said, his eyes twinkling. "If only we knew someone who could sing."

The three of them stared at Olivia.

She looked from one to the next. "I wasn't planning to sing."

Max said gently, "One last song?"

That gentle gaze of his would be her undoing. She couldn't turn him down. Still, she hesitated before reluctantly saying, "Okay." She took a deep breath.

Max was too charming by half, but it was the realization that there wouldn't be many more moments like this that sent her to the stage.

Esme, Connor, and Max cheered, while Olivia's heart pounded. Mic in hand, she shut her eyes, blocking out the pub noise and the emotions welling up inside her. Then she sang.

> Ae fond kiss, and then we sever;
>> Ae fareweel, and then for ever!
>> Deep in heart-wrung tears I'll pledge thee,
>> Warring sighs and groans I'll wage thee.
>
> Who shall say that fortune grieves him
>> While the star of hope she leaves him?
>> Me, nae cheerful' twinkle lights me;
>> Dark despair around benights me...

HER VOICE BROUGHT a stillness the pub rarely knew as Robert Burns's lyrics soared through the room. One verse in, Max joined her on the fiddle. Everything in their hearts made its way out through the music. The longing and love they'd repressed was set free.

When she finished, stillness hung in the air for a moment, then the pub broke out with applause. In the midst of it, Max's eyes locked on hers, full of emotions words could not convey. This moment would forever be fixed in her memory. Someone whistled over the applause. Olivia quickly thanked the musicians and fled to the kitchen.

Max followed. "That was... brilliant." He gave her a hug and a kiss on the forehead.

She couldn't speak. Instead, the song lyrics echoed in her mind until she was sure each word would tear her heart slowly apart. *Had we never lov'd sae kindly...* Her eyes locked on his. *Had we never lov'd sae blindly...* She had found him, and soon, she would lose him. *Never met—or never parted, we had ne'er been broken hearted.*

The stories in the songs she'd studied and sung, those of Robert Burns and others whose names were now lost, had endured because the deep emotions they conveyed came from truth. The folksongs people still gathered to hear told timeless and often tragic stories of the human condition, which people could still relate to.

When she'd sung the song minutes before, Olivia had been moved more than ever by the bittersweet love it described, because now, she understood it too well. Rather than let Max see how much, she averted her eyes. Her gaze settled upon the small window in the door to the pub. The soft lights, warm fire, and dark wood panels—things that had captivated her on that rain-soaked afternoon—now reminded her of what she would lose. Here in the kitchen, in lighting too harsh for romance, she saw a future that would end like the song.

Max lifted her chin and leaned down to kiss her.

Esme burst through the doors. "That was beautiful!" She froze. "Oh. I'm interrupting, aren't I?"

Before Olivia could answer, Max raised an eyebrow and leveled a piercing look at Esme.

Esme gestured toward the door. "I just remembered... I forgot something... out there. Gotta go." With that, she made a hasty retreat.

Max and Olivia laughed. Her amusement gave way to wistful longing to remember his sparkling eyes, the shape of his lips when he smiled, and the warmth of being enveloped within his embrace.

He circled his arms about her and kissed her forehead. "We're not parting yet." He glanced toward the pub. "Come on, lass. Let's go dance."

And they did. Max took Olivia's hand, and they maneuvered their way to the crowded dance floor. Esme leaned on the bar and watched with a wide smile on her face as they lost themselves in a flurry of twirls and laughter while music played into the night.

The night flew past until closing time, when the pub emptied. Only the three of them remained—Max, Esme, and Olivia seated at the bar, reminiscing. Olivia clung to the contentment it brought. Fleeting moments like this were the ones she would remember, simple glimpses of a life she'd come to love.

Max followed Esme to the door, locked up, and turned to Olivia. His light, carefree mood vanished with the sound of the key in the lock. From his pocket, he pulled an organza pouch and handed it to her. "Open it."

She pulled out a silver necklace with an intricately crafted rose pendant hanging from it.

"It was my grandmother's," he said softly. "I'd like you to have it."

"Max, I can't. It's a family heirloom. It should stay in the family."

"It's the rose on the pub sign. I want it to stay close to your heart." He shrugged. "To remind you of me."

To remind me of him? She didn't need a necklace.

He was already there in her heart. What she needed was something to help her forget him.

He turned her around, clasped the necklace around her neck, and whispered into her ear, "Dinnae forget me."

She turned and whispered, "I could never—"

He interrupted the thought with a kiss. Thoughts of refusing the necklace were lost in a swirl of heady emotions as a quiet inner voice tried to warn her to tread lightly. But his kiss was too warm, and his arms were too strong and safe.

Stepping back, Max slid his hand down to grasp hers. Olivia lowered her eyes and studied the rise and fall of his chest as he breathed. She wanted to bury her face in his chest and breathe in everything about him. But when she lifted her eyes, he said, "I'll walk you home."

They took their time strolling, comfortably quiet, stopping to marvel at the twinkling stars above the rooftops. Wrapping her arm around Max's waist, Olivia leaned into him as they walked down the street. So much had happened in the weeks she'd known Max. Many of the shared conversations, the music, and the missteps would be forgotten in time, but she would always remember the quiet connection between them and the sound of their footsteps as they strolled along the old cobbled streets late at night.

What if she stayed in Edinburgh and built a life with him? But that was an impossible if. She had finished the work that had brought her to Scotland. It was time to go home. That was always the plan. With a doctorate in hand, she would find a job teaching at a college or university. Her advisor had already sent her a couple of job postings for adjunct professorships. After more than a decade of working toward it, she was close to her goal. This was only a moment. The moment would pass. She'd worked too hard to get here to let this derail her.

As they rounded a corner, bagpipes played in the distance, somewhere near the castle. Perched high atop its extinct volcanic hill, the ancient fortress was lit in a soft amber hue. She felt the same wonder she'd felt the first time she saw it. But that was the magic of Scotland, a magic rooted in beauty and mournful melodies that echoed the heartache of centuries past.

They arrived at the door to her building, and he planted a dizzying kiss as he drew her closer. When their lips parted, he whispered, "You know how I feel."

"I do."

His eyebrows drew together. "You could stay here with me. We could spend every night together and wake up every morning together for the rest of our lives."

It sounded like a dream, standing here in a cool Scottish mist as if wild Scotland itself were conspiring against her.

"We could be happy together." He kissed her.

Olivia couldn't help herself as she leaned into him and kissed him as though it would never be over between them. She combed her fingers through his coarse hair and filled her lungs with his scent. But then the kiss ended, and they parted simply. But not easily.

A bittersweet smile teased his lips as he stroked her hair and her cheek. His hand slid to her neck. "Your pulse is pounding."

She whispered, "I know."

"Marry me, lass."

Every part of her longed to say yes. Her head swam with the thought. She couldn't tell him how many times she'd hoped and dreamed of it, but the answer was always the same. "Max, I can't."

With a nod, he looked away, unsurprised by her answer.

"Max?" She wanted to tell him she was sorry. She was. But she couldn't change the answer or its effect. She had hurt him—and herself most of all.

He gave her a half smile and a nod toward the door. So she turned and unlocked the door and went inside. By the time she turned back, he was on his way down the sidewalk. She watched until he rounded the corner and disappeared into the night air.

"I love you too."

19

E sme walked in from the kitchen and stopped. Max still sat at the bar, staring into his coffee. There was nothing to say that would help, but Esme couldn't just leave him sitting there. "It'll get better."

"You'd think I would have learned my lesson by now, but here I am."

Connor walked in and settled down beside Max. "Man, what happened? You look like someone stole your favorite toy."

Esme gave Connor a cautioning look as she placed his usual pint on the counter. In response to his curious look, she said, "Olivia has finished her work. She'll be leaving soon." She left out the part about Olivia rejecting his marriage proposal. The last thing he needed was their pity.

Connor nodded in understanding.

Without taking his eyes off his coffee, Max said grimly, "End of story." He stood abruptly. "I've got some errands to run." His gaze swept over the empty pub and then landed on Esme. "Can you manage without me?"

Her eyes sparkled. "I'll try."

Nodding, he headed for the door. "I'll be back in a few."

Connor watched him disappear. "Ouch."

Esme shook her head. "Aye, he's not taking it well. And she hasn't even left yet. I don't know what to do."

"There's nothing you can do," Connor replied.

Esme practically pouted. "But you're a doctor. Can you not cure him?"

Connor smiled, but it faded quickly. "There's no cure for that. He'll have to work it out on his own."

Esme narrowed her eyes. "That's easy for you to say. You've never been in love."

Connor's expression darkened. "That's not true. Maybe I haven't been in the same situation as Max, but I've loved from afar."

Esme's jaw dropped. "Really? Who?"

Connor hesitated. "It doesn't matter."

"Of course it matters! Tell me!" She leaned closer, eager to know. She stopped peering and nodded. "Oh! She's married?"

Connor wrinkled his face. "No, she's not married."

Now confused, she asked, "Then what stands in your way?"

Connor locked eyes with Esme. "Friendship."

Esme was taken aback. "Friendship? I don't understand."

Connor took a moment then explained, "If I revealed my feelings, I'd jeopardize the friendship. I couldn't bear to lose her love and her friendship, so it's better this way."

Esme's eyes widened. Her heart ached for them both. "Well, that's... sad." She muttered, "Or cowardly."

Connor barely reacted. "You're a harsh judge. Haven't you ever cared for someone without telling them?"

Esme hesitated, her gaze dropping to her hands. After a long pause, she whispered, "Yes."

Curiosity glimmered in Connor's eyes. He pressed gently, "Why didn't you tell him?"

"Professional reasons."

He wrinkled his face. "Well, that's a pathetic answer if I've ever heard one."

Her eyes widened. "Rude!"

"Aye, but true."

Without fully considering the consequences, she blurted out, "He's a regular."

Connor smirked. "A bar customer? Who is it?"

Esme averted her eyes. "Just a guy."

"Just a guy? So just tell him." He seemed awfully concerned.

Esme shook her head. "I can't. He's in here so much, if we lost his business, the place would go under."

Connor studied her. "If he's in here that much, I must know him."

She lifted her eyes to meet his and raised her shoulders in a helpless shrug, revealing a truth she'd concealed for too long. "It's you, you eejit!"

Connor's face underwent a series of transformations—shock, disbelief, and finally confusion. His eyes softened. Silence enveloped them as their unvoiced feelings became profoundly apparent.

Connor was first to break the silence. "It's always been you."

She felt breathless. "But that can't be. All those dates..."

"They weren't you."

Tears started to pool in her eyes, but anger soon replaced them. "Months..." She exhaled, fuming. "For months, I have listened... the women... so many dates..."

Connor winced. "I know. The truth is, I've never been good at expressing my feelings."

"Well, apparently, you were good enough to ask dozens of women out."

"On a dating app," Connor clarified, his voice tinged with regret.

"What's the difference?" She scowled.

"It's not real—or at least it doesn't feel that way. It's like a video game with no stakes."

"Except in the heart." She muttered, "Mine." She glared at him. "My heart is real! I'm real! Och!" She stormed off into the kitchen.

A CRAGGY old man sitting a couple of stools down chuckled. "You better go after her, lad. From where I'm sitting, it doesnae look like she's coming back." He nodded toward the kitchen, urging Connor to act.

Springing to his feet, Connor wasted no time. He burst through the swinging doors into the kitchen and spotted Esme with her back turned, shoulders hunched. He hesitated, gathering the strength to speak his mind and yet wondering whether he could. "Esme, I'm sorry.

I should have been honest with you long ago. I never meant to hurt you."

Esme turned to face him, her guarded expression barely concealing her pain. "You think an apology is enough to fix this?"

"I was hoping...?" He lifted his gaze, locking eyes with Esme. "I didn't think I stood a chance."

The anger in Esme's eyes softened. "What made you think that?"

As Connor closed the distance between them, his heart pounded in his chest. He whispered, his voice barely audible, "Because one day, it hit me like lightning. I realized I loved you too much."

"Too much for what?"

"To hope."

Esme shook her head. "Och! Well, there's no hope for you if you don't kiss me right now."

Connor's heart skipped a beat as his eyes widened in disbelief and joy. Without hesitation, he pulled Esme close and planted a kiss that left no doubt of his love. With that kiss, her body went limp against his, his only fear now the consuming power of his unleashed emotions.

As THEIR LIPS FINALLY PARTED, Esme was left breathless, her heart pounding. "Well, then. That was worth the wait." She gazed at him, smiling. "But I'm not finished with you yet!" With renewed determination, she clutched his shirt, pulled him closer, and kissed him.

The doors to the bar swung open, and glimpsing Max over Connor's shoulder, Esme waved her hand to shoo him away.

20

M ax surveyed the pub, now ready for the night's celebration. His birthday party filled him with unabashed joy. What had begun as a simple party had grown to a grand reunion of family and friends. Close family, distant relatives, and an ever-evolving group of acquaintances and bar regulars all gathered at The Red Rose for this yearly occasion. As the sun set, the historic pub came alive with laughter and conversation as multiple generations bonded over their shared love for The Red Rose. As he surveyed the collection of the people he cared for in the pub that was so integral to his family history, he was struck by the simple realization that his life was good. For years, he had grappled with his fate, but he finally saw his life from a different perspective. It felt right. He was where he belonged.

Although his father's stroke had left some lingering effects, with therapy and hard work, he had regained a good quality of life in the Highlands. He walked with the aid of a cane, and while his speech was slightly slurred, he hadn't missed Max's birthday celebrations since his stroke. Max was touched to see his father reconnecting with loved ones in his favorite place, even for just one night.

Amid the lively chatter and spirited music, Max occasionally glanced over at the bar. There, his mother and Esme were busy pouring pints and sharing laughter with his father, Connor, and a group of Connor's friends from the hospital. However, his attention kept returning to the entrance, as he hoped to glimpse Olivia walking through the door. She had yet to arrive, and it was beginning to look like she wouldn't come at all. While disappointed, Max wasn't surprised. Their last meeting had left no doubt where they stood. If Esme hadn't told him she'd spoken with Olivia, he wouldn't keep watching the door every time it opened.

As the evening progressed, Max's hope waned. To distract himself from his love-life woes, he took out his fiddle and joined the assembled musicians in playing. He lost himself in the music until Olivia arrived. Her presence illuminated the room. She'd touched more hearts than Max's through her singing and presence at The Red Rose. When she left the next morning, they would all miss her, but none more than Max.

Burdened by the thought of her leaving, he had to dig deep for the strength to get through the song. After placing his violin back in its case on a shelf above the piano, he turned to search for Olivia. Before he could reach her, a fellow musician and an old college friend pulled him aside for a chat. Despite trying to be politely engaged, Max stole glances around the room until he found her.

She stood in a corner near the kitchen, watching him intently. Max excused himself abruptly and made his way toward her. However, as eager as he'd been to reach her, he now found himself unable to articulate a single thought or feeling.

Olivia rescued him, saying, "It's quite a birthday party."

Loud laughter erupted by the bar, making conversation impossible, so they went to the kitchen.

Max grinned. "You were saying?"

She gestured toward the bar. "It's quite a birthday party."

"Aye, well, it's no longer just about me. It has grown far beyond its original purpose." His smile faded. "Look, I'm sorry about how we left things."

A wave of relief washed over Olivia. "No, I'm sorry!"

He shook his head. "It wasn't fair of me to... expect... Anyway, I'm glad everything has worked out for you."

She shook her head. "It's my fault. I think everything I did to protect myself only caused more pain for you. Or maybe I'm flattering myself. I don't know. All I know is that... I love you. I always will. But here we are. And look at all your friends. This place! This is where you belong."

With sparkling eyes, he said, "Full disclosure: some of them are family. They probably felt obligated to come."

Their smiles quickly faded.

Max furrowed his eyebrows. "I wasn't sure you'd show up tonight, but I was hoping... because I wanted to tell you... I wish I had just said, 'I love you,' and left it at that."

She nodded. "If things were different..."

"I know." Max pulled her into his arms, and they held each other tightly.

Suddenly, someone burst through the swinging doors, startling them both. Max turned to see his mother cheerfully exclaim, "Out of bar napkins! Oh, there they are. Leaving now!" With that, she disappeared.

Max and Olivia laughed, their connection still strong. Olivia said, "I love your mother."

He shook his head. "Me too."

Seeing Olivia's eyes fill with tears, Max opened his arms, and they held one another in a quiet embrace. Memories of their months spent exploring Edinburgh together flooded Max's mind, seeing his home through her eyes and falling in love in the process. Her departure the next morning would leave a void in his heart that would never be filled.

When the closeness became too much to bear, Max planted a tender kiss on Olivia's forehead and grasped her hand. "There's a party in there. Shall we go?"

She nodded, put on a brave smile, and followed him back to the bustling bar.

As they entered, Max's mother, assisted by Connor and Esme, stood on a chair to gain everyone's attention. "Malcolm would like to say a few words." The room fell into silence as Connor and Esme helped Rhona step down from the chair.

With a mischievous glint in his eye, Malcolm said, "I hope no one expects me to climb up on that chair." His smile faded as the laughter subsided.

"Max, come here, lad," Malcolm said, his voice filled with emotion. "I have watched you step up and run the family business, and I'm proud. You've done well. So…" Malcolm swallowed back his emotions, but his watery eyes betrayed him. "It's time." He handed a box to his son, and Max opened it with trembling hands. Inside, on a velvet cushion, was a key. That key represented not just a physical space but also a connection to generations past and a future yet to unfold.

Malcolm said simply, "It's the key to The Red Rose. It's yours now."

Max's heart skipped a beat. His father had entrusted him with the ownership of the pub just as his father had before him. It was not just a family business; it was a legacy. But his father believed he could do it, and that filled him with awe, gratitude, and the power of family.

A hush enveloped the room as Max locked eyes with his father. He said quietly, "I'm at a loss for words. Thank you, Dad."

Malcolm smiled warmly and clapped a hand on Max's shoulder. "Son, you have proven yourself many times over. The pub has always been a place of community. Now, it's your turn to be the custodian of this cherished establishment."

Rhona handed drinks to Malcolm and Max then raised her glass in a toast. "To The Red Rose!"

Applause and cheers erupted throughout the room in a resounding show of support for Max. Amid the jubilant celebration, Max caught sight of Olivia. She looked happy for him yet aware of the weight of that moment. Max was tied to this place and its people.

As the night wore on, Max was immersed in conversations and embraced by the love and respect the community held for him and the pub. Yet amid the revelry, he yearned to have Olivia by his side to share in this milestone and the promising future it held.

FROM ACROSS THE ROOM, Olivia felt her heart echo the bittersweet mix of joy and sorrow. In this pivotal moment, Max was embracing his destiny, and come dawn, she would face her own fate. Their journeys, having intersected briefly, now diverged.

Craving solitude, Olivia slipped away from the celebration and ventured into the cold night air. Unshed tears pooled in her eyes as she made her way home. Around her, a gentle snow fell on the cold winter's night, dusting the ground and the rooftops. Surrounded by such serene beauty, Olivia felt profoundly alone.

Ⓞ *ne Year Later*
        The lecture hall of the community college emptied quickly as students set their exams on the desk and headed out for winter break. When the last student was gone, Olivia gathered up the stack of exams and headed for her office. Once there, she closed the door, sighed, and leaned back in her chair. She'd just finished her first year of teaching.

Outside the window, large flakes of snow gently fell. It'd been snowing like this the last time she saw Max. Memories of Scotland flooded her mind as the familiar pang of regret pierced her heart. Her phone beeped, drawing her back to the present. She picked it up, read a text reminder about her electric bill, then scrolled through her social media feed.

At the top was an engagement announcement. A strange mix of emotions washed over her. He'd found someone. Good for him. She hoped he would be happy. And, good for her, she could have him. Then a tinge of jealousy crept in to trouble her. Noah had found love, and here she was, alone. With a sigh, she abandoned her plans to revise her course syllabus and instead packed up her satchel.

On the drive home, her mind drifted to Max. She remembered that feeling of being alive, passionate, and complete. She hadn't felt anything close to that since. Her life was now full; she had made it that way. Or was it only her schedule? Her heart was another matter. All that she had left of Max was the heartache, and she clung to it for the strange comfort it gave her. When she indulged in quiet moments, she wondered if he ever thought of her. What would she do if she saw him again? She was about to find out.

Once home, she ate a supermarket salad bowl then packed her bag for Esme's wedding in Edinburgh. She couldn't shake the restlessness building inside her. Max would be there. After a year of throwing herself into work with the hope of filling the Max-sized void in her life, she would see him. Her heart quickened at the thought. No matter how much she enjoyed teaching, it wasn't enough.

Her phone rang, and seeing it was Esme, she smiled. "Hello! Is this the future Mrs. Dr. Connor Begbie?"

Esme laughed. "Can you believe it?"

Olivia chuckled. "I can!"

Esme asked eagerly, "Are you packed yet?"

"My suitcase is lying open on my bed as we speak. I promise I'll be at the airport four hours early, and I've booked a lounge just in case I get through security early. When I get there, I'll dedicate my first champagne to you."

"Look at you, Miss Fancy Airport Lounge."

Olivia sighed loudly. "I splurged. Then it's off to the economy section with my blow-up neck pillow, ready to greet you seven hours later with a stiff neck and jet lag."

"Sounds lovely!"

"Doesn't it? But seriously, once I'm there, I'll be at your disposal. Whatever you need, I'll make it happen."

"It's all taken care of. There's nothing left to do but enjoy the day."

Olivia slid hangers to the side of her closet and pulled out a few items to pack. "And you still won't tell me the venue?"

"No, because it's a gorgeous surprise."

"Okay." Olivia was glad Esme couldn't see the frown on her face. Why Esme felt the need to surprise her was a mystery, but Esme was quirky.

"So, mainly, I called to let you know that one of us will pick you up at the airport."

"No, you won't. I'll take a taxi to my hotel. I've booked it for the previous night, so I can check in as soon as I get there."

Esme didn't sound convinced. "Well, that's nice that you've got your hotel booked, but a taxi?"

Olivia laughed. "Yes, a taxi. It's a twenty-minute ride. I'll be fine. You've got more important things to do, like be crazy in love and get married."

"Well, okay. I've got that covered, at least. If you change your mind..."

"I've got your number."

"Fine, be that way. Can't wait to see you!"

"Me too!"

And she couldn't wait. But she also couldn't help but feel a twinge of envy. Esme had found her happily ever after, while Olivia wondered if she ever would. There she was again, thinking of Max. She heaved a hopeless sigh and resumed packing. *It's been a year. He's moved on.* Her stomach sank. If Noah had time to get engaged...

THE RED ROSE pub was lively as always as people chatted and laughed, savoring their drinks and the cozy ambiance. Max moved behind the bar, skillfully serving pints and engaging in friendly banter with his customers. But despite the busy scene, he paused and stared off to the distance. Esme guessed what was on his mind. The musicians were playing a song that Olivia had sung. A year had done little to get her off his mind. He barely mentioned her name anymore, but in moments like these, Esme knew he thought of her. But today, he would see her, and she feared it would open the wound.

Connor walked in with a mischievous grin, waving an envelope in the air. Esme perked up, wiped her hands off with a bar rag, and rushed to him.

"Is that it?" Her eyes gleamed with curiosity.

Connor grinned and handed it to her. "The marriage schedule," he declared with a dramatic flourish. "Which means it's official! Sorry, lass, but there's no turning back. We'll be wed in a week."

Esme's eyes widened with excitement, and she snatched the envelope and extracted the contents. Her eyes swept over it as she read the details. "It looks real."

Connor nodded, and their eyes locked.

Max came down to their end of the bar to pour a draft and glanced at the paper. "What's that?"

Esme quickly slipped it back into the envelope and gave Max an innocent smile. "Oh, nothing," she replied nonchalantly. "Just some paperwork for the wedding."

Max nodded and left.

Connor gave Esme a puzzled look. "Why the secrecy? Is there anyone here—or in the city, for that matter—who doesn't know you're getting married?"

Esme wrinkled her face as she surveyed the crowd. "I'm not sure. Should we have a show of hands?" She laughed, but it was hollow.

Connor grew suspicious. "What was all that cloak-and-dagger about the marriage schedule?"

Esme raised her eyebrows. "What? I don't know what you're talking about. But I should get back to work."

Connor narrowed his eyes. "Esme..."

She hesitated then relaxed her shoulders in defeat. "Well, okay. Olivia is listed as a witness, but I haven't told Max."

"Why not?"

With a guilty expression, she said, "I was afraid he might back out of the wedding if he knew she'd be there."

Connor looked doubtful. "Would he?"

She leveled a tolerant stare. "Not everyone holds their feelings as close to the vest as you do."

Connor frowned.

She hastened to add, "Which is fine, as long as I know what they are."

Connor tilted his head. "Well, you may have a point. But if I'm honest, I would've expected Olivia to back out if anyone did. That's a long trip from America just for a wedding, and knowing Max would be there might be too much to bear."

Esme nodded.

He raised an eyebrow as he peered closely at Esme. "But she's coming because you didn't tell her."

Esme's jaw dropped. "That's not true. She knew Max would be at the wedding. What she doesn't know is that the wedding party is a total of four, and the only guests are our parents." She felt increasingly guilty.

Connor slowly shook his head. "You let her think she was going to be part of a large wedding..."

Esme nodded reluctantly.

"So she could get lost in the crowd and avoid a confrontation with Max."

"*Confrontation* is a pretty strong word. They parted as friends."

Connor leaned back and eyed Esme frankly. "Friends don't sneak out of parties and catch an earlier flight without saying goodbye."

Esme bit her lip. "Yeah, that was rough on Max. Saying goodbye would have been harder."

Connor said gently, "So you lied to your two closest friends."

She frowned. "You make it sound so..."

"Dishonest?"

Esme rolled her eyes. "Och! Well, I had to do something."

He winced. "Did you?"

Esme sighed. "I want them to be as happy as we are."

Momentarily charmed, Connor's eyes softened. "I

know you meant well. I just hope it doesn't blow up in your face—and our wedding."

"It won't. Fingers crossed. Can you not see they're in love?"

Max called her name from the opposite end of the bar.

"The boss is calling." With that, she escaped Connor's scrutiny. While she wouldn't admit it to Connor, she had the same doubts and fears. While neither Max nor Olivia were prone to dramatic outbursts, she decided, for the sake of the wedding, to give them a couple of days to get used to each other.

OLIVIA GOT out of the taxi, checked into her Edinburgh hotel, and promptly collapsed onto the bed. Three hours later, her watch alarm woke her. When she landed, she got a text from Esme, asking to meet. She was due at The Red Rose in an hour. A shower and two coffees later, she was almost awake. Her nerves made up for her lack of sleep.

Come on, Olivia! We knew this was coming. But no amount of preparation seemed able to stop her heart from racing.

On a typically chilly December afternoon, Olivia stepped out of her hotel, bundling up to stave off the biting wind, but cold dampness seeped into her bones. Gray clouds hung low in the sky, casting their gloom on the city. As she walked along cobblestone streets, wind whistled through the closes and wynds, carrying a faint hint of the sea.

Edinburgh's historic buildings stood tall and stoic,

their aged stone façades darkened by the city's history, while the soft mist turned to drizzle and painted a sheen on the cobblestones.

Looking especially quaint, the shop windows twinkled with fairy lights and Christmas decorations. An occasional burst of warmth spilled onto the streets from inviting cafés, where people had found refuge in steaming mugs of coffee or tea. Even in December, Edinburgh held an enchantment for her unmatched by anyplace else—perhaps even more so in winter. It made the warmth and cheer of cozy cafés and pubs even more pleasing. With each step, the charm of the city seeped into her soul.

As she approached The Red Rose, vibrant Christmas lights cast a welcoming glow through its windows as familiar sounds of laughter and music spilled out onto the street. She opened the pub's wood-framed glass door, and a wave of warmth enveloped her. The aromas of a wood fire and pub grub filled the air and mingled with the cheerful chatter from a few scattered tables. An overwhelming sense of belonging caught her off guard. From the start, the place had been a cozy sanctuary for her, but the friendships she'd forged and the memories she now cherished were dear to her heart. It felt like she had come home.

22

From behind the bar, Max glanced up. Tension spiked, charging the air. Esme stepped in from the kitchen. Her usual chatter halted as she looked between them, wide-eyed.

"Hello, Max," Olivia managed.

Max's mouth worked a moment before her name broke free.

Feeling uneasy under his dark gaze, she tried to flash a casual smile, but it was fleeting. "I'm here for the wedding."

His eyes never left hers as he nodded. "It's good to see you." His voice was barely above a whisper.

A flutter of warmth rose in Olivia's chest, and she echoed softly, "It's good to see you too."

Esme punctured the quiet with her boisterous voice. "Well, don't just stand there. Come here, give us a hug!" After guiding Olivia to her regular spot by the fire and promising her a drink, she leaned close to Max. "Don't just stand there like a statue. Get over there."

Max slid into the seat opposite Olivia. "Sorry. It hardly seems real."

"I know." Her eyes dropped to her hands knotted on the table.

His fingers grazed over her bare ring finger. "No ring?"

"No." Feeling uneasy, she added, "I've been busy."

Max leaned back, eyes drifting to the table. "Me too. Very busy." He lifted his eyes with a piercing intensity that made her shiver.

She averted her eyes, surveying the paneled walls adorned with vintage photographs and antique sconces. Without the evergreen garlands strung up for Christmas, it could've been any day from their past. "I like what you've done with the place."

His grin was warm. "That's all Esme—for the wedding reception."

Amid the silence, a tide of emotions ebbed and flowed between them. Soft music began in the background, thanks to Esme, who'd just paired her phone playlist with the sound system. She meant well, but the romantic strains heightened the tension. Olivia battled an urge to lean over and kiss Max—an impulse she vowed to suppress. It was only nostalgia, a ghostly remnant of what used to be. But the charm of the pub, once so beguiling to her, was her enemy now.

A soft chuckle from Max broke her reverie.

"What?"

"Do you remember the first time you came into the pub?" His smile threatened to break into a full laugh.

"Go ahead. Laugh. No one looks their best in pounding rain with no umbrella."

His eyes sparkled. "You looked... adorable."

She rolled her eyes. "Right."

His gaze lingered on her. "Your wet yellow hair pulled back into a bun. I thought..." He stopped, smiling to himself.

"You thought what?" For a moment, she'd almost relaxed. "Maybe I don't want to know."

His expression shifted to serious. "Probably not." He paused. "But there was something about you."

The air was thick with unspoken words. Olivia tried to lighten the mood. "It's the accent, wasn't it? Upstate New York. Gets them every time."

His laugh was genuine. "Aye, that must be it."

Max's gaze softened, the flickering flames of the fireplace reflecting in his eyes. "It feels like yesterday... and a lifetime ago."

Olivia was teetering on a precipice. When she got on the plane, she'd had a plan. There were bound to be unresolved feelings between them, but she'd been convinced they would fade into friendly nostalgia. But now, here with Max, her mind raced with unforeseen possibilities. And The Red Rose was a silent accomplice, offering comfort while she lost her heart.

A pair of bartenders arrived and were greeted by Esme. Max excused himself and joined them to give instructions for the evening, but Esme hooked her arm in Max's and drew him back to Olivia's table.

"Sit down, Max. The lads can take it from here. I need you to keep Olivia company while I run home and shower off the beer smell."

Olivia thought she detected some reluctance, but Max sat down.

Esme dug through her purse. "Connor's meeting us at the restaurant." She pulled out her keys and shoved them into her pocket. "Hold on." She went to the bar, poured two pints, and returned. "This will take the edge off the jet lag."

Max squinted skeptically. "I don't have jet lag."

She smirked. "No, yours is just to take off the edge."

Olivia said, "After this, I might lapse into a coma."

"Either way, you'll have a relaxing evening."

Olivia laughed and shook her head.

Esme waved. "This is me leaving. I'll be back in twenty minutes." She turned to go but stopped. "Unless... Max, why don't you walk Olivia to the restaurant?"

Olivia must have looked as surprised as she felt, because Esme said, "Oh, didn't I tell you? Max is joining us. See you there! Bye!" And with that, she was gone.

Max winced. "Sorry. Esme's..."

"Being Esme?" She should have suspected Esme would try to bring them back together. "Look, Max, I'm fine. The restaurant's a short walk away. I'll make excuses..."

"No, you won't. Because I'm going." His insistent mood shifted. "Those two aren't married yet. Someone's got to chaperone them."

Warmth filled her heart at the typical Max-like gesture. Although she'd intended to keep some distance between them, she looked forward to an evening with Max.

Max flashed a grin. "With those two, it'll take both of us." He winked and excused himself to disappear through the swinging doors to the kitchen.

While Olivia waited, several musicians straggled in and set up. By the time Max reappeared looking showered and shaved, wearing clean blue jeans and a muted green Shetland wool sweater, the music had begun. The evening crowd gathered to bring the pub to life with familiar laughter and exuberant conversation.

Max stood before her. "Ready?"

Olivia nodded and stood. Together, they walked to a Rose Street restaurant. As the four reminisced with more laughing than talking, a year of longing and uncertainty melted away to reveal the same bond she and Max had once known.

Max walked her home. With one free day before the wedding, Olivia succumbed to his persuasive suggestion to spend the next day together. She could hardly have refused when he stood at her door under the moonlight and pleaded, "For auld lang syne?"

In the morning's clarity, she rationalized her decision. They'd had a year to sort through their feelings, which had to have changed. Hers hadn't, but his probably had. Besides, it was only a day.

OLIVIA STEPPED OUTSIDE, full of anticipation for her day with Max. Edinburgh's charming streets were just coming to life, and the winter air tingled with excitement. It was as if she and Max had made a silent pact to stop time and savor each moment.

Their first stop was a cozy café nestled inside a close. They sat by a window, sipping steaming cups of coffee and sharing warm pastries. The conversation flowed effortlessly as they reminisced about old memories and caught up on what they'd missed in each other's lives.

Max took her hand, and they strolled down the Royal Mile, exploring shops as if they were tourists. Christmas had cast its magic over the town. The streets and shops twinkled with festive decorations. They strolled through a bustling Christmas market as aromas of mulled wine mixed with roasted chestnuts. When they grew cold, they ducked into Olivia's beloved Edinburgh Central Library for a warm rush of nostalgia then crossed the street to the National Library of Scotland. It was there that, while taking in an exhibit, their hands touched, and their fingers entwined.

With Olivia's jet lag in mind, Max had made an early reservation for dinner. Whether it was the quiet intimacy of the restaurant or their long day together, they grew quiet, as if they'd run out of words to say. Or perhaps they no longer needed words. Olivia feared it was the latter. Yet she couldn't stop herself from basking in his presence. Once he touched her hand, she was lost. It was only a moment that was over too quickly. They didn't touch again, but it was all she could think of.

After dinner, they stepped outside, and Max kissed her, first on the cheek then the lips. "I'm sorry."

"I'm not." She couldn't help how she felt. Hiding it seemed pointless.

Max's face lit up. "I've wanted to do that all evening —all day, if I'm honest."

Olivia smiled but averted her eyes. She hadn't made it more than a few steps before she turned, grabbed his shoulders, and pulled him to her for a kiss. This time, they poured their hearts into that kiss until some guys from a wandering stag party yelled, "Oi! Get a room!"

Max and Olivia laughed and strolled back to The

Red Rose. Max touched base with the staff then glanced about the crowded room. He tilted his head toward the kitchen, took Olivia's hand, and led her through the kitchen and up the stairs to his flat.

As the strains of a ballad drifted up to Max's flat, they danced. Resting her head on his shoulder, she breathed in the scent she'd missed. Outside, a clock chimed midnight.

She whispered, "Time's up." With one look at Max, her smile faded.

His intense gaze only mirrored what her pounding heart felt. This was the moment to leave, but she let it pass. The music played on, but they'd stopped dancing at some point. She tightened her grip on his sweater, pressing closer, and kissed him with a year's worth of longing. Her plans and all rational thought melted in the warmth of his arms and the heat of his kiss, a slow burn she'd lost the will to fight.

So she didn't. She took his hand and led him to the bedroom.

23

The afternoon sun shone golden through the gothic windows in The Witchery's guest suite, where the wedding was set to take place. Named for the thousand people burned for witchcraft on Castlehill during the fifteenth and sixteenth centuries, the site now served a happier purpose. Living up to its magical name, the rooms were enchanting. Adorned with rich drapes, ornate antique furnishings, and dark carved wood paneling and brocade-papered walls, it was like something from a fairytale. Beyond the sumptuous sitting room was a separate bedroom with a four-poster bed draped in velvet and clothed in fine linens. It was desperately romantic.

Olivia and Max had to scramble to sneak Olivia out in time to go back to her hotel to get ready. When Max picked her up at her hotel to take her to the wedding, she took one look at him in a kilt and entertained thoughts of skipping the wedding.

She and Esme now waited behind the closed

bedroom door of the suite, while Connor, Max, and the bride's and groom's parents waited in the sitting room.

Standing back to take in the vision before her, Olivia sighed. "Look at you!"

Beaming, Esme lifted a couple of layers of her fluffy tulle skirt and made a face. "Too *Swan Lake?*"

"No. Too gorgeous!"

Esme had made a stunning transformation from her usual jeans and Doc Martens to a breathtaking bride. She wore a vintage ivory dress with an off-the-shoulder V-neck and a wide satin ribbon cinching the waist. From there, layers of tulle cascaded down to a classic tea length.

Olivia, in her maroon stretch velvet knee-length dress ruched at the waist, opened the door to the sitting room just a crack. Both sets of parents were chatting with Connor, who, along with Max, looked dashing in kilts.

Max, who'd been waiting nearby with the minister, leaned closer. "Ready?"

Olivia turned to Esme, who gave her a wide-eyed nod. After giving Max the go-ahead, she waited until the others were seated. With his phone at the ready, Max started a playlist Esme had prepared, and it played through hidden speakers. To the tune of "My Heart's in the Highlands," Olivia stepped into the sitting room and took her place opposite Connor and Max. Then Esme entered and stood beside Connor.

The air was charged with quiet anticipation as the two said their vows. With no warning, an emotional flood washed over Olivia. A clear vision of her standing with Max as his bride made her head swim. Then the vision was gone. There could only be one explanation—

she was losing her mind. The next minute, Esme and Connor were married, and there were hugs all around.

She glimpsed Max grinning. "What is it? Lipstick on my teeth?"

He laughed. "No, I was just doing maths, wondering how many combinations of hugs there could be among eight people—not counting the minister."

Olivia murmured, "He doesn't look like a hugger."

Max frowned. "No. But more importantly, when do we eat?" He raised an eyebrow. "For some reason, I didn't have time for breakfast."

Olivia smiled as she recalled why.

Max's question was answered when a knock at the door revealed a room service attendant with two carts for high tea. Olivia thought this must be the perfect way to get married—relaxing in glorious surroundings with close family and friends. That was how she wanted hers. She shuddered inwardly. *Where did that come from? It's just the wedding. People get weird at weddings.*

When they'd finished their tea, Esme lifted her champagne glass. "Here's to family and friends. Thank you all for sharing this perfect wedding with us. Now off you go to The Red Rose for a rowdy reception! We'll be close behind you." But when the parents weren't looking, Olivia caught the couple exchanging a mischievous look.

THE RED ROSE was bustling with more energy than usual. Closed to the public for the special occasion, the place was already packed when the wedding party arrived. Max had hired ample staff so he could take the night off.

When the festivities were in full sway, Max took a turn at the mic and raised his glass. "Ladies and gentlemen, let's raise a glass and gather round to celebrate the grand occasion of Connor and Esme's wedding! As the best man, I've a few words to share.

"Now, we all know Connor here is a man who can diagnose just about anything, except his own love life. It took him a while to realize that the cure for his heartache was standing before him. But good things come to those who wait, or in Connor's case, wait a wee bit too long.

"Connor, my friend, you're not just an outstanding doctor, but you've found the perfect prescription for happiness in Esme. And, Esme, you've stolen Connor's heart so completely that even his stethoscope can't detect it.

"As we gather in the magnificent land of Scotland, surrounded by ancient castles and misty glens, we can't help but feel the magic in the air. So let's raise our glasses to Connor and Esme. May your love be as heart-warming as Connor's bedside manner..." He raised an eyebrow. "And as enduring as Esme's patience while waiting for him to make a move." He winked at Esme. "Here's to finding true love. May your journey together be a wonderful adventure! *Slàinte Mhath!*"

The guests echoed, "*Slàinte Mhath!*"

Max worked the room while Olivia caught up with some friends. As the band played a ballad, he found her sitting at a table nestled in the corner, looking as though the remnants of jet lag had caught up with her.

As soon as he was able, he joined her. Sitting down,

he pointed to Esme, who was dancing like no one was watching, while Connor could barely keep up. "Opposites do attract. There's your proof."

"Pardon?"

"I said... Never mind."

Olivia squinted and pointed to her ear. "I can barely hear you."

Max opened his mouth to speak but realized it was futile. He stood and beckoned her to follow. They went through the kitchen, but instead of stopping, he continued up the stairs to his flat. As he walked through the door, he asked, "Can I get you anything?"

"No, thanks. I'm good."

"When I saw you huddled in that corner—"

She frowned. "I wasn't huddled."

He smiled. "I thought you might like a quiet moment."

Olivia drew in a breath and exhaled. It was pointless to deny it. "I've had a busy few days."

Max's gaze swept over her soft hair and satin-smooth skin. "You know," he confessed, leaning closer, "I've spent a lot of time thinking about you."

A soft smile danced on Olivia's lips as she met his gaze. "I've missed you too."

He opened his arms. "Come here." He'd missed having her in his arms. When they were together like this, he knew in his soul they belonged together. But he'd said all he could, short of begging, and he wouldn't do that. All he could do was hold her in his arms and love her. He slid his hand through her hair and kissed her.

A voice rang out from the stairs. "Max!" A knock sounded.

With a groan, Max leaned back. "Hold that thought." He went to the door and found the new bartender looking sheepish.

"Sorry. The beer's too foamy. Esme said to get you because she's not going down to the cellar in her wedding dress."

"I'll take care of it." Max shot a helpless look over his shoulder to Olivia. "Stay here as long as you like. We'll talk later."

On the way to the bar, he met Esme in the kitchen. "I heard. Foamy beer."

With a dismissive nod, Esme asked, "Where's Olivia? I saw you two leave."

"Upstairs."

Esme's eyebrows furrowed. "Is she okay?" She started up the stairs, but Max touched her arm to stop her.

"She's fine. She just needs a few minutes."

"Why?" Esme scowled. "What did you do?"

Max laughed and raised his hands in defense. "Nothing. There's nothing to look at here. Move along."

With a doubtful look, she asked, "Are you sure?"

Max leveled a look. "Aye."

When she'd finally accepted his assurance, she turned away then turned back. "I just remembered what I came in here for."

"What?"

"You."

With a mischievous glint in his eyes, he said, "Sorry, lass, but I dinnae fancy married women."

She leveled a withering look. "Remember when you proposed to Olivia?"

Max stared in disbelief that she'd chosen her

wedding reception to reminisce about his broken heart. He said wryly, "Aye, sounds familiar."

She looked at him with pleading eyes. "You're both still in love. Don't let this chance slip away."

"It's not up to me."

With a stern look, she said, "Ask her again."

Connor ducked his head inside the door and grinned. "There you are. I thought you'd done a runner."

She laughed but turned to Max long enough to leave him with stern parting words. "Do it, Max!"

As OLIVIA HEADED DOWNSTAIRS on her way back to the reception, Max's mother greeted her.

"Oh, hi, Rhona." She felt the need to explain. "I just needed a minute. Max offered his flat."

Nodding with understanding, his mother said, "Sometimes you just need a break from the noise. I used to sneak off for wee two-minute breaks. It works wonders."

The tea kettle clicked off. "Care for a cuppa?"

"Yes, please." While Rhona poured, Olivia said, "You know, I don't even drink tea usually, but it's in keeping with the rest of my day. Nothing feels usual." She rolled her eyes and shrugged. "It's the jet lag." But it wasn't the jet lag. She'd felt off-balance emotionally all day. She blamed the wedding. And Max.

Rhona leaned back on the counter, sipping her tea. She looked up, a knowing smile playing on her lips. "Weddings have a unique effect on people."

Something about Rhona's gentle manner put

Olivia at ease. She'd felt it as soon as she met her on that idyllic day in the Highlands with Max. The memory brought an overwhelming surge of emotion, and the threat of some tears, to her eyes. With a light laugh, she said, "Apparently, I'm one of those wedding weepers."

"It's okay," Rhona said, concern clear in her voice.

Olivia almost believed that it was. "I'm sorry. I'm really not like this. Ever." She tried to put on a bright face but failed pitifully.

Rhona nodded understandingly. "Weddings are like that sometimes. Come, have a seat."

Olivia gratefully accepted the invitation, sinking into one of two wooden chairs at a small table by the door.

They didn't speak at first. Rhona looked completely at ease, but Olivia felt compelled to break the silence. She couldn't hold it in anymore. "It's not jet lag or the wedding. It's Max."

Rhona didn't look a bit surprised.

Olivia shrugged, but her voice trembled. "I love him."

Rhona's gentle smile almost put her at ease.

"There. I've said it." Now the floodgates were open. "I've tried not to. I've planned my entire life—doctorate, career... everything. My life is in America, and his life is here."

"What does Max say?"

Olivia smiled. "Your son is amazing."

Rhona smiled. "I think so too. But that doesn't answer my question."

Olivia fought back the tears. "He says he loves me."

Rhona seemed far more at peace with the news

than Olivia was. "We knew when he brought you to meet us."

"Was it that obvious?"

Rhona shrugged. "A mother can tell." She took a thoughtful sip of her tea, her soft gaze tempered with wisdom. "Love is a precious thing. It has the power to change our lives in ways we never thought possible."

Olivia nodded politely. She appreciated Rhona's attempt to help, but love didn't have the power to change her life.

Rhona was gentle but resolute. "You have plans and dreams. That's important. Look what you've accomplished already! It says a lot about you."

"Thanks." *So I should be happy. But look at me.*

With an encouraging smile, Rhona said, "The unknown is daunting. But life has a funny way of working things out."

A sliver of comfort crept into Olivia's heart. She wanted to believe it, but she'd never been comfortable with things out of her control.

Rhona reached across the table and patted Olivia's hand. "If Max is the one, you'll both find your way. Love's a journey. You can make all the plans that you want, but... there's an old saying: 'Man plans, and God laughs.'"

Olivia leaned back with a sigh. "Thanks for talking me down off the ledge."

Rhona smiled warmly. "You weren't on a ledge, just a crossroads. Stop and rest for a bit, and you'll figure it out."

Max stepped inside the kitchen and, seeing them, raised an eyebrow. "What are you two up to?"

Rhona laughed and got up. "Nothing, just solving

the world's problems over a cup of tea." As she passed Max, she gave his arm a squeeze, then she disappeared through the swinging doors to the pub.

WITH ESME'S URGING ringing in his ears, Max made a decision. The stakes were too high to let the woman he loved slip away. But he hadn't expected to find her in close conversation with his mother. It almost seemed like an omen, as if she were meant to be part of the family. But she wouldn't be if he didn't ask her. But not in the kitchen.

If she kept gazing at him with those luminous eyes, she would render him speechless. His pulse quickened as Esme's words echoed in his mind. *Do it, Max!* This was the moment. "Come with me."

"Where?"

He took her hand and led her up to the flat. Olivia eyed him with a puzzled expression, which made him smile. "We need to talk."

Once upstairs, he led her to the window that looked out at the castle, awash in gold light. "It's a braw view, is it not? I haven't tired of it yet." *And I hope you won't either.* He took her hands in his and drew them to his lips.

Olivia's phone rang. Max flinched.

With an embarrassed shrug, Olivia pulled her phone from inside the neckline of her dress. Her eyes widened when she saw the screen. "It's from work. Sorry." As she went to the opposite end of the room, she glanced back over her shoulder. "It's still afternoon there." Then she stopped. "Hello?"

In an instant, she was all business, listening, thoroughly focused.

Wishing he couldn't overhear, Max stared out the window. He glanced at his watch. In New York, it was the end of the workday, but here, it sounded like it was the end of his dream.

The conversation didn't take long. When it ended, she pressed the button and slowly made her way to a sofa and sat. "I can't believe it."

Max had surmised more than he wanted to know. Still, he went over and sat beside her. "What's happened?"

She looked both elated and confused. "Instead of bringing me back as an adjunct professor, they've offered me a full-time tenure-track position."

"But that's good, is it not?"

"Yes." Olivia laughed. "It is! I just can't believe it." As her laughter trailed off, her eyes saddened. "It's what I've worked for. But it feels like the end of a road."

To persuade himself as much as Olivia, Max said, "It sounds great."

She looked surprised. "Yeah, it is."

It was all he could do to be positive. "You deserve it. After all your hard work, it's worked out for you." *But not for me.* Unexpected anger arose from within. He had known it would end this way, but he'd allowed his own desperate hope—with Esme's help—to convince him to try again. This was madness. He had to let go.

When he was younger, he might have run off to America with some romantic notion of making it work, but his life now was here. Even before his father had passed the pub along to him, he had not only reconciled himself to this life but also embraced it. After watching his friends graduate and move on with their lives, he'd come to realize that the university degree he'd sought with such fervor was only a means to an end. Living a rewarding life was the goal, and he was living that now, just as generations before him had. And Olivia was living the life that she wanted. He wanted that for her too, but it was breaking his heart.

He needed to leave before he said things he shouldn't. "I'd better get back."

She averted her eyes. "I need a minute to think."

He couldn't look at her now without revealing too much. "Sure. See you down there."

When he was halfway to the door, she called out. "Max? Did you want something? When you brought me up here?"

He shrugged. "What? Oh... No. Just the view."

He headed downstairs. *And to marry you.*

24

Over the rooftops of Edinburgh, dawn was breaking. Shoes in hand, Olivia sat on a barstool while Max said goodbye to the last of the guests.

He turned to her. "Come on, I'll walk you home."

Having abandoned her hotel room the previous night, Olivia said, "Or I could crash here." Her smile quickly faded as she saw his reaction. "If... you wanted me to, which you... don't. Max, what is it?"

With a heavy sigh, he said, "It's late. Let's get some sleep."

He didn't enjoy seeing the pain in her eyes, but he was too tired to pretend nothing was wrong.

Olivia nodded slowly. "Okay. I'll just... put my shoes on, and I'll be out of your way."

He didn't mean to, but he snapped, "I said I'd walk you home."

"I know. But you're not very good company."

"You'll be free of my company soon enough." He went to the door and leaned on it, waiting.

"Yes... but I thought we might spend my last day here together."

"Did you? I thought you'd book an earlier flight to get back to that job." As soon as the words were out, he hated himself for sounding bitter and petty.

Olivia had every right to be angry, but instead, her gaze softened. "I was always going to go home. The job didn't change that."

With a cynical laugh, Max said, "Yeah. That was the plan. Wasn't it?"

QUIET HUNG in the early-morning air as they arrived at Olivia's hotel. She'd deluded herself into thinking they could be happy, if only for a few days. What she got was a heartrending kiss and embrace to mark the end of everything they'd been to each other.

Max took a step back. "Congratulations on the job, Olivia. Be happy." But nothing in his voice conveyed his words' meaning.

She mustered a quiet goodbye and went inside. She was finally leaving the crossroads Rhona had spoken of. She had lingered too long, but a new path lay before her. The future she'd dreamed was within her grasp, but without Max, her achievement felt hollow. She would miss seeing him at the bar with his tousled hair and the way he would smile when he caught her watching him work. But it was his last kiss that would haunt her, for it held the quiet acceptance of their paths diverging. He'd already let go, and she wished he hadn't.

Once inside her hotel room, she felt stifled. She

stood at the window, unable to bear Edinburgh's charm because Max was too much a part of it. As she looked at the Old Town, canopied in gray skies and thin wisps of clouds, a wave of sadness washed over her. She had to leave.

THE AIRPORT LOUNGE guests and staff bustled about as the murmur of conversations ebbed and flowed. Olivia sat alone. The past few days had been a roller-coaster of emotions—wedding joy, reuniting with Max, and then parting. That stabbing wound would stay with her.

She stared blankly into her coffee as Rhona's words echoed in her mind. *"If Max is the one, you'll both find your way. Love's a journey."* She'd forgotten to mention what an arduous, turbulent journey it was.

The prospect of life without Max cast a stark light on her once-alluring career, now devoid of the fulfillment it'd once promised.

Olivia's thoughts were interrupted by a woman who sank into a seat behind hers. Disapproval laced with regret marked her phone conversation—that and volume. It wasn't hard to surmise the family drama in progress.

"But divorce? That sounds a bit drastic."

That was more than Olivia needed to know, but she'd just gotten a coffee, so she planned to finish then change seats.

The woman sighed. "Love, he was married to his work before he married you."

A brief silence followed, during which Olivia

wondered, *If she has to share half a conversation so willingly, why not just put the dang thing on speaker?*

Olivia scanned the lounge for a better seat while the woman said, "But work matters. It's people's identity. What are we without work?"

That was one of the saddest things she'd ever heard. People were more than their jobs. But the thought soured as she finished her coffee and settled into a comfy chair by the window. Her own life was consumed by work. In the past year, what had she done other than work? But the first year of a job was always like that. As the dust settled this year, she would focus on her work–life balance.

Her plane was boarding, so she headed for the gate. Bound for home, she was newly resolved to find time for a personal life, time to be happy. She hadn't been unhappy the past year. But as she tried to think of the times that she'd truly enjoyed what she was doing, all those times were in Scotland.

The line progressed steadily until she reached the gate and headed through the jet bridge. Scotland had been an extraordinary time in her life, but there would be others. She put her carry-on bag in the overhead compartment and sat.

But, no matter what lay ahead in her future, Max wouldn't be there. With Max, she felt alive. When she was struggling with her research, he filled her days with laughter and hope. And her work was better for it. She relaxed and lived life, and she sang. She'd forgotten how much she loved singing. Not that she didn't enjoy teaching. She did. But when she sang, Max was there. Having him in her life invigorated her, and it carried over into everything that she did. Max made her life complete. No job would ever do that for her.

As passengers filed down the aisle, uneasiness tugged at Olivia's heart as her life came into clear focus.

"Excuse me." Olivia stepped into the aisle, got her bag down from the overhead compartment, and annoyed the last few boarding passengers as she headed upstream to the cabin door. After stopping briefly to tell the flight attendants she'd had a family emergency and wouldn't be reboarding, she headed for customs and the exit beyond. The voice of reason insisted that this was impulsive, her dream job was waiting, and most of all, she had plans! She ignored it, though. Her heart didn't care because it wanted Max. Who was she to deny it?

Snowflakes fell, heavy and silent, as Olivia headed out of the airport and rolled her carry-on suitcase to the first taxi in line. The twenty-minute ride took an eternity, but she was undaunted. The driver was chatty, with a thick Glaswegian accent she worked to decipher.

"How long are you here for?"

"I'm not sure, actually."

"From America, are you?"

"Hmm? Yes." She'd never met a Scottish taxi driver she didn't enjoy chatting with, but today, her thoughts were elsewhere.

"Whereabouts?"

"New York."

He smiled. "Brilliant."

"Upstate, not the city. Still brilliant, but cleaner air and less traffic."

He asked, "Have you been here before?"

"Yes, this morning, actually."

He cast a questioning look in the rear-view mirror.

"Change of plans. Long story."

His furrowed eyebrows somehow made her feel obligated to explain. "Actually, it's a short story... involving a man."

"Och!" He nodded then glanced at her through the mirror with crinkling eyes. "A Scotsman?"

She couldn't help but smile. "Yes."

"Well, that explains it." He rounded the corner, and there they were, in front of The Red Rose. "Good luck, lass!"

Olivia thanked him, grabbed her suitcase, and got out. As the driver pulled away, Olivia stepped up to the entrance, her heart in her throat.

What have I done?

She drew in a breath, exhaled, and pushed on the door. It was locked. She tried it again. Still locked.

This was not the scene that had played in her mind. With a glance at her watch, she realized the pub wouldn't open for another hour. Max would be upstairs in his flat, sipping a steaming mug of coffee, while she froze down here on a chilly December morning. If she called him, would he even answer? She headed down the close to the kitchen door and rang the bell on the intercom. He didn't answer.

They hadn't parted on the best terms. Still, he wouldn't sit upstairs and leave her on the street like this. *He must not be home.* Was it possible he'd closed up shop and gone away for the weekend? He'd never done it before, but the pub was his now. He could do what he wanted.

That left her alone in a foreign country with no place to stay. Esme and Connor were off in Spain on their honeymoon, so they were no help. And with

Christmas a week away and Hogmanay a week after that, the hotels in the area could well be fully booked.

Now you've done it.

Before a full panic set in, she pulled out her phone and thought about calling Max. Instead, she started searching travel websites for rooms.

"Olivia?" Yards away, Max stood staring in surprise. With hesitant steps, he closed the gap between them. "What's wrong?"

"Everything." Olivia glanced away, struggling against a tide of emotions.

Max's expression shifted from alarm to restraint, as if he'd remembered their last encounter mere hours before. "What is it?"

"I was on the plane, but..." Olivia hesitated, suddenly unsure of herself, then she blurted it out. "Do marriage proposals expire?"

Max looked away for a few moments, his eyebrows raised as if trying to understand what was happening between them. "Probably at some point."

Unable to read his expression, she averted her eyes. "So I guess a year's probably too long."

"Probably."

"Oh." She wasn't sure how to react. But when she looked up again, a faint glimmer in his eyes filled her with hope.

He smiled reassuringly as he nodded slowly. "Although, once it expires, the party can make a new offer."

"Really?" Olivia looked away. She could hardly believe what she'd heard him say. But he didn't appear to be joking or trying to tease her.

Frowning, she leaned back skeptically. "That isn't

one of your weird Scottish laws, is it? Like being against the law to sing on trains?"

His eyebrows drew together. "Oh, the train law is real."

"Good to know. And the other?"

"If you marry me, I'll tell you."

His sudden earnestness caught Olivia off guard. "Really?"

He laughed. "You seem awfully eager to know about Scots law."

"Not that! I mean, do you want to get married?"

With a sudden earnest expression that took her breath away, he said, "Well, since you asked, yes, I do." He spun her around. Then they kissed, unaware of the snow gently falling about them.

EPILOGUE

One Year Later

The windows outside The Red Rose glowed with warm light. Inside, low chatter peppered with soft chuckles and the clinking of glasses filled the air with cheer. Max's birthday party was in full swing.

Amid the joyful chaos, Connor sat comfortably at the bar, a six-month-old baby nestled in the crook of his arm. Esme breezed in from her evening class at the university, set her backpack next to the diaper bag, and coached a new bartender on the art of pulling the perfect draft. Across the room, Rhona emerged from the kitchen, double doors swinging behind her, with a tray full of golden-crusted pie slices. She served them to her friends then sat down to join them. Nearby, Max and his father debated the greatest Scottish golfer of all time.

A cold gust rushed in as Mary McNabb arrived and gave her former flat sitter a warm hug. Olivia drew her to a window table, where their smiles and soft conversation caught up on lost time.

Max appeared at Olivia's table and stole her away. Stepping onto the stage, Max cradled his fiddle while Olivia took her place at the mic stand. Her clear soprano rang out, bringing the room to a hush.

O my Luve's like a red, red rose
    That's newly sprung in June:
    O my Luve's like the melodie
    That's sweetly play'd in tune!

As fair thou art, my bonnie lass,
    So deep in love am I:
    And I will love thee still, my dear,
    Till a' the seas gang dry:

Till a' the seas gang dry, my dear,
    And the rocks melt with the sun;
    I will luve thee still my dear,
    When the sands of life shall run.

And fare thee weel, my only Luve,
    And fare thee weel a while!
    And I will come again, my Luve,
    Tho' it were ten thousand mile.

THE RED ROSE continued to flourish as it had through the centuries, a testament to the enduring power of human connection. Within its walls, Max and Olivia had embarked on a journey together, so different from what they'd once planned, and so much better than they'd ever dreamed. It began as a simple escape from the rain on a gray Scottish day. And now she had found her way home.

Next from J.L. Jarvis:

This Christmas, a young woman is about to find out wishes can come true — but in the most unexpected ways.
Once Upon a Winter

THANK YOU!

Thank you for reading! If you enjoyed this book, please consider leaving a review or a rating. Your feedback on bookstore, Goodreads, and Bookbub websites helps other readers discover books they'll enjoy.

instagram.com/jljarvis.writer

facebook.com/jljarvis1writer

x.com/JLJarvis_writer

youtube.com/@jljarvis-author

goodreads.com/jljarvis

bookbub.com/authors/j-l-jarvis

ALSO BY J.L. JARVIS

Waterfront Summers

(Can be read in any order)

The Cottage at Peregrine Cove

The House on Serenity Lake

Moonlight on Mariner's Bluff

Drake & Wilde Mysteries

(Reading Order)

Love in the Time of Pumpkins

Secrets in the Hollow

Shadow of the Horseman

Standalones

(Can be read in any order)

A Cowboy Kind of Love

A Christmas Eve Stop

Christmas by Lamplight

A Kiss in the Rain

App-ily Ever After

Once Upon a Winter

The Red Rose

Highland Vow

Short Stories

Highland Passage

(Can be read in any order)

Highland Passage

Knight Errant

Lost Bride

Highland Soldiers

(Reading Order)

The Enemy

The Betrayal

The Return

The Wanderer

American Hearts

(Can be read in any order)

Secret Hearts

Forbidden Hearts

Runaway Hearts

For more information, visit jljarvis.com.

Get monthly book news at news.jljarvis.com.

ABOUT THE AUTHOR

J.L. Jarvis is a left-handed former opera singer/teacher/lawyer who writes books. She now lives and writes on a mountaintop in upstate New York.

jljarvis.com

www.ingramcontent.com/pod-product-compliance
Lightning Source LLC
Chambersburg PA
CBHW030324200626
46816CB00006BA/1913